The Test

Even the book morphs!
Flip the pages
and check it out!

Look for other **ANIMORPHS**® titles by K.A. Applegate:

ANIMORPHS®

The Test

K.A. Applegate

AN
APPLE
PAPERBACK

SCHOLASTIC INC.
New York Toronto London Auckland Sydney
Mexico City New Delhi Hong Kong

The author wishes to thank Ellen Geroux for her
help in preparing this manuscript.

For Michael and Jake

Cover illustration by David B. Mattingly
Art Direction/Design by Karen Hudson/Ursula Albano

ISBN 0-439-11517-5

12 11 10 9 8 7 6 5 4 3 2 1   0 1 2 3 4 5/0

Printed in the U.S.A.
First Scholastic printing, July 2000

CHAPTER 1

My name is Tobias. Still a freak of nature. Part human. Part bird. Confused? Don't worry, it gets better.

I am flying over the forest. The air is thick. A storm is approaching. It is only early afternoon, but the sky is growing black as the front moves in on the city. A towering wall of rain, wind, and cumulus clouds.

I had to find food before the storm. I was hungry. But then, I'm always looking for food. That's life for a bird of prey. Hunger.

A shrew stepped out from its burrow. It loitered nervously, sniffing the moisture. We had the same thought, me and the shrew. Hunker down against nature's wrath, but fill your belly first.

I was higher on the food chain. I tucked into a dive.

My wings pressed tight to my body. Air whistled past. Mountains, forest, and sky. All a blur, a flashing streak. Everything but the shrew, shifting agitatedly, chomping on a seed . . .

My talons struck, embedded, and squeezed. Drained life instantly.

Wonder what it's like? Dig your fingernails into a too-ripe peach. Rip sections off with your teeth. Gulp them without chewing. The kill is something like that.

I downed the shrew and lifted off.

I don't think about the kill anymore. I'm hawk and human. I'll explain later. Just try to understand that the hawk must feed the human. It has to happen.

I don't think about it anymore.

That's a lie.

"You vile little bird! Do you realize what you've done? Do you realize what you've become? You're trapped! You have to live out your life as a bird!"

Her name was Taylor. My Yeerk torturer. Her voice screeching. Bruising my ears. Tormenting me after every kill. Other times, too. Still, after all this time . . .

THWOK! THWOK! THWOK! THWOK!

A helicopter! Hovering low over the trees, dispersing terrified crows in all directions. If I were a true hawk, I'd have cleared out with the other birds. Instead, I circled around and flapped toward the turbulence.

My friends, the Animorphs, the ones who fight the Yeerk invasion of Earth, say that since my capture, I live too much of life in my head. They must be right. I'd almost missed everything.

Not just the helicopter. The humans below, streaming across rough forest floor, the tires of their ATV's scoring the soil. The searchlights streaking the trees in the daytime darkness, making rabbits and deer dart in alarm.

I flew to the nearest ranger station. It was ringed by squad cars and TV news vans. I swooped down, closer to the action. Landed on a low branch. A blond woman in a raincoat held a microphone close to her lips and swatted wind-whipped hair away from her face.

"Bobby McIntire," she shouted above the noise of the vehicles, "missing now for two full days since he wandered away from his camping party. Hope that he'll be found alive is fading. But it's not just a race against time and the weather." Lightning struck the sky above her, imparting urgency to her words. "Little Bobby is deaf and can't hear the desperate calls of rescuers. Kelly King," she concluded, looking sky-

3

ward, "reporting live." She held a frozen, concerned expression until the producer gave her the all clear.

"I will break you." It was Taylor's voice again, whispering in my mind. *"You can't win."*

I set a course for the storm front. A strange thing to do, to turn toward the lightning. To fly into the line of rain, the thunderclaps, the wind.

But it made me feel like Lindbergh over the Atlantic. Fearless and strong. Maybe even a little heroic.

I wanted those feelings.

See, it wasn't long ago that the Yeerks captured me. A crazed and insane human-Controller made my life a hell for several excruciating hours. I survived. I even thought the torture was over. I didn't realize that torture doesn't end when you're freed.

People think it does. People who've never been through torture think that when the physical injuries heal, you're healed, too. They're wrong.

Torture plays tricks on your mind. "You're weak and scared," it says. "You think you're in control? Hah!" it says. "Doubt yourself. Worry, and question, and fear," it tells you.

Pain can be very convincing.

Sometime during my capture, my mind was

assaulted with memories, images of all the times I've been weak. Or think I might have been . . .

Like my first time at the Yeerk pool.

My mind flashed back to it now, to the scene at Yeerk Central, that echoing underground dome with a sludgy pool churning at its core. The Yeerk pool. That's where the Yeerks do their dirtiest dirty work, where parasitic, sluglike aliens dunk your head in the muck and force one of their kind through your ear.

The Yeerks squeeze your brain and wring out your freedom. They control all thoughts and movements. They silence your howls and screams of grief until you are nothing but a slave. A stupid puppet. An unwilling soldier of the Yeerk Empire. A threat to all humanity.

But you've probably heard about all this by now. Right?

Tha-BOOM! Boom!

A thunderclap roared and half brought me back to the present. The other half of me was still at the Yeerk pool that first, horrible time. Clinging to the rock face, praying for camouflage, searching the colossal cavern for a way to escape. A way to get past Visser Three's men.

<Where's Tobias?> I'd heard Rachel say, faintly.

How long since I'd morphed to red-tailed

5

hawk? An hour and fifty minutes? An hour and fifty-five?

How long?!

The others had escaped already. The other Animorphs, I mean. They'd dodged the visser's fireball gauntlet. They'd slipped out to safety, back through the janitor's closet, back into the school. Rachel, Cassie, Marco, Jake.

Had I missed the deadline? Had I been more than two hours in morph?

Couldn't have. Can't have. No. I'd be trapped forever. A bird.

Independent, free, alone.

Forever.

Images of the human life I'd led till then flooded my mind. The images were dark. My apathetic aunt. My alcoholic uncle.

Then, something brighter, something powerful surged through my mind. Something else. Shoring me up. Drawing me in. A wave of . . .

What? What had I felt then, at that moment, with the seconds ticking down? With the deadline chasing me . . .

Weakness or strength?

"You'll never know," Taylor said. *"You won't know who or what you are when I'm done with you."*

Bobby McIntire needed to be found.

I let a fading thermal lift me into the atmosphere.

My name is Tobias. I'm a human. I'm a hawk. If you want to find something in the forest, you'd do well to ask me.

There's nothing I don't see.

7

CHAPTER 2

Tha-BOOM! Boom!

Thunderclaps. I let the warm air draw me up. Three hundred feet. Higher. I could see through the haze, from city's edge to the mountains.

The national park is a very big place. You could hike for days and never see anyone. Spotting a boy from a helicopter would be like finding the needle in the haystack. And the haystack was about to get really wet.

Binoculars, infrared goggles, and laser sights flipped on. I don't mean to brag, but nature gave me excellent tools. I can see a hiker's broken shoelace. A robin's chicks.

I can pick out deer poop.

"You vile little bird!" Taylor's voice, always humming in my ear.

Quiet as a glider, my personal search plane swept huge, broad strokes above the trees.

My friends, the other Animorphs — the other kids who knew the great Andalite warrior Elfangor, who'd been there as he died, and who'd accepted the Yeerk-fighting Andalite technology to become any animal they can touch — they were expecting me to show up at Cassie's barn. There was a meeting scheduled for after school. If I wanted to make it, I had to travel east.

I edged west, following the search party's tire tracks. Tracing the lines as they crossed and converged in a half-mile section of sparse tree cover. I was guessing that this was the last place the boy was seen. Good place to start. I dove to fifty feet, skimming the treetops, looking for a sign, a clue. Anything.

Nothing.

A raindrop struck my wing. No, not yet! Three more drops hit me like BB's.

A whistling gale pushed me back into the air and blew me away from the search party tracks. I flapped harder to fight the strengthening wind. It was pushing me toward mudflats. Forcing me toward a dried up stream.

The raindrops were starting to feel like wargame paint pellets. I remember. My uncle took me to do the paint-ball thing. I hated it, but it was one of the only things we'd done together.

Anyway, I was going to have to stop. The down-pour was starting.

Suddenly — a splash of red against brown. A shred of bright cloth caught on a bramble.

Yes.

<Bobby?> I chanced in open thought-speak. <If you're here, show me where you are.> Brushing the treetops, I scanned the mud. Nothing.

The wind was absurd. Violent one minute, dead the next.

Then — a single footprint. A kid's footprint.

<Bobby!> I called again. <If you can hear me, wave. Or move. Do something!>

A faint rustling of brush. Then, more movement. I circled in to land. A dirt clod shot straight up into the air, grazing my beak.

<Whoa, okay! Great, Bobby. Good work.>

I didn't see the giant sinkhole until I almost landed in it. It was a pit so invisible under the overgrowth, it would have taken searchers months to find it.

I peered down at the kid. He was searching wildly for the source of my voice. His eyes were swollen from crying. His hands were raw from trying to climb up the vertical, featureless sinkhole wall. He stood in stagnant water a foot deep. And a flash flood was on the way.

<We're gonna get you out of there,> I said. But I didn't have a morph that could haul him

out. Hork-Bajir? I wasn't practiced enough with the blades not to lacerate the kid and I definitely couldn't let him see an alien. <Hang tight, Bobby. I'll be back soon. It'll be okay.> A lightning bolt sizzled the ground nearby. Not good.

The trip to the ranger station was probably the worst flight of my life. The rain pummeled me. The wind screwed up my feathers. But the very worst part was the dead air. By the time I reached the ranger station, my body was burning ligaments for fuel.

Through the windows I saw most of the search party, inside and drying off. Getting ready for another round of wet and nasty searching. Then I saw a guy who looked like he needed a miracle. He was sitting outside on a stump, letting the rain drench him through. The ink from his name tag was running down his chest, but I could still read the letters. "Mr. McIntire." Bobby's dad? He fixed his sad stare on the mountains.

I touched down just feet from him. Didn't once think about the consequences. <Listen,> I said, <I know this is going to sound crazy. I know you'll think you're losing your mind. But I can take you to Bobby.>

You can tell a lot about a person by the way they respond to a talking hawk. There's the run-away-screaming type. The bring-palms-to-head-to-squeeze-out-demons reflex. Even the kill-the-animal maneuver. Most people don't do too well when their reality's challenged.

But Bobby's dad was cool. I mean, he looked kind of freaked at first. His eyes bugged out and he spun around frantically, looking for the prankster who was fooling with him. But once the initial surprise faded, he quickly regained his composure.

"Okay," he said. "Lead the way."

He probably thought he was nuts, but I don't think it would have mattered whether he was hearing voices or talking with aliens. He just wanted his son back.

That kind of love . . . it made me feel . . . strange.

I flew from tree to tree, a few hundred feet at a time, waiting for Mr. McIntire and three rangers he'd convinced to come along. All the while I gave him directions in private thought-speak. At least I could stay a good distance from the men, to keep it uncertain whether a hawk was really running the show.

I pictured Bobby in the pit, the torrential rain funneling into channels, forming a raging arroyo. Racing like a hungry, deadly snake. A massive, silent snake that Bobby's deaf ears wouldn't hear.

"You will die, Andalite." Taylor's hateful voice, droning in my head.

<Over the hill,> I directed.

Then we crested the rise and I saw something I didn't think was possible. Sheets of rain punished the earth to our right and our left, but over Bobby's sinkhole . . . unbelievable. A corridor of rainless clouds with two ends of a weak rainbow marking the borders.

I was sure my mind was making the scene up. It couldn't turn out this well. Nothing ever did. Taylor wouldn't let it . . .

<Bobby!> I called. I pumped my wings and found him, the water rising around his knees. I perched on a low branch and watched as three powerful rangers pulled him to safety. Watched as Bobby collapsed in his dad's arms, shaking, as joy replaced fear.

Bobby's dad glanced up at me, gratitude in his eyes.

Ever have something work out so perfectly, you feel you could fly? That's how I felt — and the cool thing was, I could actually do it. I could actually fly.

I took off down the swath of rainless sky toward Cassie's barn. It felt so good. I played in the air like a pilot at an air show, awed the audience with my death-defying stunts. I cut my engines, fell into a nosedive, ready to pull up just seconds before I hit the ground.

And then . . .

13

A golden eagle, twice my size, screeching toward me like a wrecking ball . . .

WHAM!

And all was blackness.

I never even had a chance.

CHAPTER 3

"This hawk's gonna feel that wing. Hero or not, when he wakes up, he'll hurt like crazy."

My eyes snapped open. Through the links of my cage I spied the faces of two concerned, lab-coated veterinarians. Both women. One brunette, one blond. The words *University Clinic* were stitched on their pockets.

"Do you think Superbird needs an epidural?"

I tensed my extremities. Right wing not responding. A sore and twisted neck. That nasty golden eagle had banged me up pretty bad. The memory of the impact got my hawk heart pumping. Fear, territoriality, confusion.

"No, I gave him enough medication to keep him comfy till morning. Hey, look, he's awake.

15

Feeling better, Mr. Hawk?" the blond one said, with the gentle condescension appropriate for wildlife who can't make it in the wild.

I could have found both vets extremely annoying. But as it was, with an ugly vulture in the cage next to mine, and a prehistoric egret two doors down, I was actually glad to hear a human voice.

How much time had passed? What day was it?

"Seen the headlines?" the brunette asked me, as if in answer to my question.

Sometimes, not always, if you ask questions you want answers to, the universe will respond.

It was the evening edition newspaper that she held in her hands, and it confirmed that I'd been asleep way too long. "'Father Claims Hawk Led Searchers to Lost Boy.'" She smiled at me, then summed it up.

"You da bird!"

The vets chuckled. They didn't know this was no laughing matter. They didn't understand . . .

It hit me, right at that moment. I'd messed up big time. That headline . . . the kiss of death . . . if the Yeerks found me first . . .

I was stupid. So stupid!

Any time you get an animal doing unusual stuff, you get Yeerks. To Yeerks, all animals are suspects, possible "Andalite bandits" disguised in morph.

This was bad. What was I thinking?

My friends, they'd be looking for me, too. I'd endangered our own security. By trying to fight Taylor's ghost, I'd dragged my friends into danger.

Stupid. Weak.

I had to morph! Morph and get out before . . .

But no. I couldn't morph in front of the vets. And there were video cameras, mounted up in the corners of the lab, recording everything.

Who'd get to me first?

"What's he doing? Flapping his wing? Hey, he's gonna get hurt. Chloe, quick! We need to sedate him."

Sedate me?

I fell back to the floor of the cage and lay motionless.

No way would I be sedated.

Not with two groups looking for me. Two groups I knew would take that headline very seriously.

Group One: my friends.

Group Two: my enemies.

"Wait," the vet said. "Forget it. He calmed down. He's fine. I don't know what that was about."

"Okay, Superbird. Stay out of trouble. We'll see you in the morning."

They were going away? They were leaving me here!

Why did everyone leave? Why . . .

They walked to the door, switched off the main fluorescent overheads, deadbolted the door behind them.

They were going home. They had homes to go to.

They were leaving me to face my fate alone.

The room was cold and sterile. Sick and injured birds squawked and cooed in the partial darkness.

Alone.

And all I could do was wait.

CHAPTER 4

Sccreeeeech!

The sound jarred me from a restless half-sleep. I looked at the clock: 1:12 A.M. Scanned for the source of the sound.

For a moment, glowing metal blinded my sensitive hawk vision. When my sight returned, the lock on the door was sizzling. Evaporating . . .

Behind the door, heavy, punishing footsteps slammed down the hallway. A sound that meant only one thing.

Hork-Bajir.

The door burst open.

Tseew! Tseew!

Seven-foot-tall bladed bodies charged into

19

the room! Video cameras disintegrated in flashes of Dracon fire.

No time to morph!

I pressed myself to the back of the cage. Tried to cover my reddish tail, tried to pretend I wasn't there.

They were on me instantly, scowling with fiery eyes. Holding weapons to my head.

"You mine, Andalite!" asserted the Hork-Bajir with the worst breath. "Visser Three will give praise."

This guy obviously hadn't been on Earth very long. Getting praise from Visser Three would be like trying to stop a brushfire with a glass of water. But I wasn't about to burst his bubble.

He hefted my cage into the air and ran for the door, banging me roughly. His henchmen, two in front, two behind, surrounded him. Their weapons were drawn, their eyes were searching. They were tense as we moved into the hall. On guard. Almost as though they expected . . .

Tseew. Tseew.

Three humans appeared twenty feet down the corridor. Their Dracon rounds ricocheted off the walls.

What was going on?

Humans firing Dracons at Hork-Bajir!

Controller versus Controller?

"Drop the bird," a man with a mustache ordered. *"Now!"* The Hork-Bajir snorted a laugh at the wiry man. "Bird is visser's. You rebel make mistake." Quick as lightning, he raised his arm and opened fire on the humans.

The human-Controllers were agile and dove for cover. They just weren't agile enough. An abbreviated scream echoed down the hall. The mustached man vanished in a flash of light and heat, a silhouette scorched against the whitewashed wall. The other humans didn't seem to notice the loss of their comrade. Or else, they didn't care.

Only Yeerks can lose a teammate and not bat an eye.

BLAAAAM!

Four more humans coming up from behind! Slamming the Hork-Bajir before they knew what hit them.

I didn't know who to root for. Hork-Bajir or human? Visser Three or . . . who? Who were these people?

A long, sharp, Hork-Bajir blade caught my cage and lifted it. He ran swiftly toward the exit. This guy could move! Smashed over a stainless steel medical cart. Crashed into empty cages stacked against the wall.

Blocked!

Three more people! Large ones, dressed in dark leather, with straps and metal clasps covering their bodies. Bodies that blocked the exit.

My captor halted, claws screeching across the polished floor.

He turned back and moved toward a window. Three new Dracon-packing people moved in to block his path.

Surrounded!

My cage dangled precariously from the Hork-Bajir's blade. Aliens and humans froze in a grim, momentary standoff.

Suddenly, my captor leaped at the smallest person. A woman. It was a low move, a desperate attempt at escape. Foolish, too. The others were on him instantly.

We crashed to the floor, my cage caving beneath the Hork-Bajir's weight until the cold steel bars pressed tight against my feathers. Around me swirled a sea of hands and claws, clutching wildly. For me. The prize.

I couldn't keep track of what happened next. I just know that someone sent the cage careening across the floor. My frail, injured body tumbled like a rag in the dryer. The cage lodged under the large sink of a utility closet, my hawk body even more bruised and damaged.

I heard frantic shuffling from the fight beyond, but from my position, I could see very little. Deafening Dracon fire was followed by a momentary stillness. Heavy footsteps marched my way. Four Hork-Bajir feet came to a halt before my cage.

"Gafrash!" one roared. A hideous appendage reached for me. I cringed, waiting to be taken again, waiting to be seized.

The Hork-Bajir arm jerked back.

The feet tensed and turned to run, but there was nowhere to go.

Because four more feet, twice as large, gigantic and familiar, landed with a thunder-thud.

Rachel!

One Hork-Bajir was down. The other snatched up my cage.

<Oh, no you don't!> Rachel cried, baring her massive, flesh-tearing teeth. Her wild grizzly bear claws flashed like giant steel rigatoni and lashed my captor's arm.

<The cavalry's here, Tobias,> she huffed. <Hang on!>

23

CHAPTER 5

"Gafrash horlit!"

The Hork-Bajir let go. My cage hit the floor with another painful crash.

<Get Tobias!> Rachel cried.

Marco, in gorilla morph, was the only one with an opposable thumb, an often undervalued appendage. He reached for me, but a downed Hork-Bajir grabbed his leg and yanked him backward.

So Rachel nudged me with her massive front paws, pushing my cage across the floor, down the hall, away from the fight.

Suddenly, the cage stopped. We'd run into something. We'd hit human feet.

Rachel froze, sniffing the air hard. I looked

up. Sleek, suede boots. Fashionably worn jeans. The torso and head were in shadow. Who was this? Some innocent vet student, trapped by the battle?

Her arm appeared from behind her back. Her fingers clutched a Dracon beam . . .

My heart stopped.

The girl's fingers glistened and sparkled in the semidarkness. The way real flesh fingers never do.

<Taylor,> Rachel hissed, her voice rough with rage.

"Make one move, bear, and your next stop is the taxidermist."

<Yeah, right!> Rachel leaped, claws slashing.

Tseew!

Taylor seared a hole in Rachel's flank.

"HhhhoooRRRAAWWRRR!" Rachel dropped, groaning with pain.

And Taylor grabbed my cage with her artificial hand. The hand she had accepted in exchange for her freedom. Taylor's story was a sad one. A story of a girl who'd lost her face, arm, and leg in a terrible fire. The Sharing, the Yeerk front organization, had been there for her. Offering her a new face and arm and leg. All she had to do was agree to be infested. A voluntary Controller. All she had to do was let a vile gray slug wrap around her brain. But the Yeerk that infested Taylor was nuts. Taylor had pretty much lost it, too. Not a very stable situation. And there I was.

I couldn't believe what was happening. My torturer had captured me. Again.

No.

The fingers of her real hand poked through the bars of my cage, threatening to touch me as she lifted the cage right up to her face.

NO!

She didn't speak a word but her icy stare said it all. *Thought you'd seen the last of me, Andalite fool? Well, you thought wrong.*

Taylor straightened her pearly, plastic fingers. I knew what she was going to do. I'd known since the moment I recognized her in the shadows.

"I love surprises," she whispered. And without any further warning, snowy particles frothed from the fingertips of her prosthesis.

Gas!

She was gassing me just like the time she'd captured me under the grounds of The Sharing's new community center. In moments, I'd be paralyzed. The only difference was that she didn't realize I was the same "Andalite" she'd previously captured. I could only hope she didn't remember.

I stretched out my talon. I gripped the fleshy fingers of her real hand. Then I closed my eyes, shut my ears, shut it all out. The animal screams, the grunts, the human shouts. The horror of reliving a nightmare.

Acquire her. Acquire her. Become her.

A nauseating idea. Necessary.

I clutched her fingers tighter. To Taylor, it must have seemed like a pitiful attempt to fight back, but she didn't know the truth. She didn't know that I felt her DNA flow into me. Felt her body relax, slacken under the acquiring trance.

The gaseous powder stung and tingled, pricking my skin like invisible nettles.

But Taylor, too, was immobile! Paralyzed! For an instant, I'd slowed her down. Incapacitated her.

Not enough. Not nearly enough.

My talon went limp. My body fell numb. Taylor's eyes buzzed back to life just in time to watch me realize that this gas was different from the stuff I'd experienced before.

"Version 2.0," Taylor laughed. "Enough general anesthetic to knock you out completely."

Blackness rushed in from all sides as my vision dimmed.

<Rachel?> I called weakly. <Jake?>

If they answered, I didn't hear them.

Why me? What had I done to deserve this? Foolish questions, useless self-pity . . . I was a warrior.

27

All I could do was look straight ahead. Into the dismal depths of Taylor's mad, hypnotic eyes.

In that moment, I saw clearly. I saw that I was just a blob of mud bobbing through the raging stream of her thoughts. The stream couldn't be stopped and it would destroy me.

It would break me apart.

CHAPTER 6

Skrrr-eeeek!

The sound of a metal spoon dragged across the bottom of a pan. The smell of canned tomato soup warming on a stove. These ordinary things drew me out of darkness. I opened my eyes.

I was still caged, but now there were half a dozen Dracon beams aimed at my head, clamped to my cage with vises. Not high-tech mechanisms fresh off the Yeerk drawing board, but the kind of clamps you pick up at Ace Hardware.

It didn't matter. Point was, I didn't have any hands. My captors knew that hawk beak and talons couldn't unscrew anything.

Blinking beneath each mounted Dracon was a red light. A sensor? I didn't move. I didn't dare.

29

The thought of more torture set my bones knocking. I couldn't take any more.

I started to tremble, uncontrollably. I watched the sensors with both minds, hawk and human. Each had been almost destroyed and both parts of me remembered . . . the pain, the hopelessness! Impossible to escape . . . red light, blue light. Agony . . . endless . . .

Morph. I could morph to something small and crawl away. Undetected. Steal away. *Do it, Tobias. Do it.*

"Morph, my friend," Taylor warned, her voice cold and confident, "and the beams will fire automatically."

I hadn't seen her there, sitting at a kitchen chair, mug in hand, sipping soup.

I'd felt her, though. Her evil had a way of dominating the very nature of a room, of coloring everything around her and stoking my fear.

I couldn't escape. I never really thought I could. Not then, not now. Taylor was back, just as I guessed she would be.

"The computer controlling the Dracon beams is sensitive to basic changes in shape. You cannot escape."

Wait. That wasn't true. I could escape. I could morph. Morph and die!

"Yes, you could choose death," Taylor said, answering my thoughts. "I've deliberately given you that option." She paused to take a slurp of soup, her eyes still fixed on me.

I looked at the kitchen, and at the small, shoddily built, low-ceilinged structure. Something was definitely wrong with this picture. Yeerks choose the best. They take the best of everything we humans have, and when the best we have to offer isn't good enough, they use stolen alien technologies to make it shine. This was . . . what? Some sort of hovel. My cage rested on a Formica table scarred with cigarette burns.

"Choose death," she repeated casually, "or . . . listen to what I have to say." She rose, dropped her mug in the sink of the strange little kitchen, and returned to her seat. "I have a deal for you, Andalite."

She was so casual. Not the Taylor I'd known.

What trick, what scheme did she have up her sleeve?

"Good," she said, seeing that I'd decided to postpone death. "It would be much harder to solicit help from an Andalite who's dead."

Help?

Yeah, and Rachel will pass up a sale at Express, Crayak will win the Nobel Peace Prize, a Yeerk slug will turn down a promotion.

What did she have up her sleeve?

"Civil war is coming, Andalite," she began. "Yeerk versus Yeerk. We've had enough of the petty visser fights, the favoritism, the punishments . . . the Council makes us sick."

Anger flushed her face. She'd said the last sentence with such vehemence that for a fleeting instant, I knew I could believe her. The Council *did* make her sick.

But then, her guard went up again. The spark in her eye made her look part politician and part actor, part trial lawyer, and part scheming teen-aged girl. It was a face shrouded in lies.

"The Yeerks must move on as a race," she continued. "The time has come." She got up again and opened the ancient refrigerator. "We need to make a civilization with the hosts we have." She glanced at me. "Many of us realize that the eternal wars have to end and that the loss on Leera, the stalled offensive on Earth, and now the apparent bungling on the *Anati* planet have discredited the current leadership enough that it cannot survive."

She pulled a bag of carrots from the fridge. Seriously bizarre. She was talking political strategy while she snacked. Like we were hanging out at her house after school, planning the rigging of the homecoming queen election.

She continued. "We want to be more like you, Andalite. We need a structure that will transform us from rebels to leaders. We want to be more like Andalite society. Even more like the humans." Her teeth snapped a crisp carrot in two. Her eyes stared at me. "We want to move toward democracy and we need your help to do it."

It was like the world's weirdest press conference.

I didn't believe a word she said.

Not a word.

So I tested her. <I suppose all you need from me are the names and locations of the remaining Andalite bandits? You know, as a token of my co-operation?>

Taylor laughed. She was a violent, aggressive, and ruthless personality. Personalities don't change. Not much, anyway. I waited for her to prove me right. I waited for proof that she was still working for Visser Three. That this talk of rebels was all a ruse.

"Nice to hear your voice again, Andalite. The Andalite with the power to stay in morph for more than the two-hour time limit. Your voice brings back such sweet memories." The tone in her voice set me shaking again. "I learned a lot about you during our time together, Andalite. I saw your mind. I saw your courage dribble away. I would enjoy finishing you now. Breaking you." She slinked toward my cage. "Right here and right now. You think you're strong, but I know you're weak. It would take seconds!" She paused just enough to let the thought rattle me. "But this time, Andalite, it's your cooperation I require. I need you and your fellow Andalites. I need you to help me destroy Visser Three."

She wasn't working for the visser. She was out to destroy him. That's what she'd said.

Unguarded anger seethed from her face. If she was lying, it was impossible for me to tell.

"You've fared badly as a bird." She looked at my bandaged wing, at my matted feathers, my twisted neck. "You have Visser Three to thank for that. His Hork-Bajir aren't big on gentle."

She wanted me to become angry, too, and take revenge, get back at the visser, join forces with her . . .

"Don't answer now." She pulled a scrap of paper from her pocket and pushed it through the bars of my cage. "Here." It was a Web address. "Talk things over with your comrades and leave me a message there. Sign it 'Bandits.'"

Then she unlatched the cage door, threw open the nearest window, and disappeared behind a curtain, leaving her dirty dishes in the sink.

CHAPTER 7

The red sensors flickered out.

I hobbled from the cage, hopped to the window. The ground was a few feet below me. I fell outside. Taylor. Visser Three. Civil war. Weakness . . .

She'd let me go.

It was too much to sort out. I needed my friends. I needed Rachel.

I dragged myself into the shadows, morphed and demorphed to repair injuries. Injuries which by this time were so painful they bordered on torture themselves. I lifted off. Free, but my mind was weighted.

As I rose into the air, I saw the place I'd been held. An old trailer, parked by a junkyard. A rebel hideout. Far from the city and the Yeerk pool. Could she be telling the truth?

I flapped toward town, toward the lights, toward Rachel's. Over buildings topped by digital dishes and cell phone relays. Suddenly, I cut the gas, strained my wings, dropped to a roof.

If she weren't telling the truth, if she were feeding me lies . . .

She'd have planted a tracking device on my body. Of course! The Yeerks were tailing me. I was bringing them straight to my friends. Straight to the Andalite bandits.

When I'd finished kicking myself, I picked the smallest morph I had. Flea. I focused on the tiny blood-sucking body.

SCHWOOOP!

The roof rushed at me. Slate shingles became slick and huge as glaciers. My vision fractured like light through a prism and my hearing cut. It was all about the other senses. Taste, smell.

Feeling. I waited for the corner of a tiny chip to bust out of my skin. Any tracking device would fall away from a flea's body. It would prove that Taylor's words were meaningless. That I could write her off forever. I wanted to.

I grew smaller and smaller. Nothing snagged, nothing stretched my stretchable skin. Nothing bulged from my body. No global positioning chip. I was unmarked.

Okay. Okay. No easy answers. Just complications.

I demorphed and rocketed past streetlights, car headlights, and neon signs to Rachel's house. Her window was open. I shot through and planted my talons on the bedpost, swishing my feathers as I came to a stop. She jolted out of sleep.

"Thank God!" she whispered. I fluttered down next to her. She touched me gently. A smile filled her face, then was replaced by rage. "That jerk!" Her voice hardened. "That scum."

<I'm okay,> I said. <Taylor let me go.> I felt safe in Rachel's presence, but my voice still sounded raw.

"We searched for you for hours. I wanted to kill her."

<I think I wanted you to.>

"What's her deal?"

<She wants to work with us,> I said. My words sounded preposterous. I wondered for a second if I hadn't dreamed it all. <It's weird. She says that if we give her help, she gives us Visser Three.>

"Don't believe it," Rachel muttered, charging out of bed. "C'mon. Let's get the others."

An hour later, we had all assembled in Cassie's barn.

"A deal?! Come on. Our help?! Puh-leeze. If

37

some Yeerk contracts a democracy virus, I'm supposed to care?" Marco said skeptically. "I don't think so."

<I agree with Marco. I do not think her telling the truth is likely. We cannot forget that she was a sub-visser. She rose to her position by being ruthless. I do not believe the Yeerk,> Ax nearly sneered.

"But what if she's telling the truth?" Cassie countered. Cassie was the only one of us who'd befriended a Yeerk before. Who'd actually morphed a Yeerk. I knew she, at least, would want to give my story some consideration. "Maybe she really does believe in a better way. She wouldn't be the first Yeerk to have a change of heart."

"No, she'd be the last. That creep wouldn't even breathe if it didn't serve her," Rachel sneered. "She's not about to found a democratic leadership because it's a just philosophy. She wants something else."

"Seems obvious to me," Marco answered. "It's the means, not the end, that interest her. She's keen on democracy because it's a process that will eject Visser Three."

"Do you always assume the worst of people?" Cassie asked.

"Always." Marco smiled. "People are who they are. My bet is that when Taylor failed to break Tobias with torture, the visser sent her packing. She's probably been plotting revenge ever since."

For a second, nobody spoke. Jake glared at Marco and I was pretty sure I knew why. I was guessing it was probably also the reason no one had mentioned how I'd been recaptured in the first place. No one had mentioned that I'd made a huge mistake by rescuing the lost kid. Now I realized why. Marco'd mentioned torture, something he was apparently not supposed to do when I was around, not even in passing.

Their hypersensitivity made me mad. Did they think the memory would mess me up? Couldn't they see me getting stronger? Couldn't they tell I'd be fine?

"Tobias, what's your take?" Jake said, breaking the silence. "You know more about her than anyone."

What was my take, now that I wasn't locked in a cage, waiting to be tortured? Rachel looked at me. Her eyes gave me strength.

<Power,> I said, suddenly knowing the truth. <Power is the one thing in the world I know Taylor wants. Using me to get Visser Three must strike her as irresistible irony.>

"Know what would be even more irresistible?" Marco added. "Get Visser Three and the Andalite bandits both killed in the process. Two birds, one stone."

Rachel nodded. "Marco has a point. An irony in itself."

"We've had other chances to get Visser Three and we've blown them," Jake said. "We might not get a shot like this again. Can we afford to pass it up?"

<Civil war means Yeerk against Yeerk,> Ax observed. <It means confusion, betrayal within enemy ranks, a foe distracted by internal strife. It is a unique opportunity.>

"Right," Marco agreed. "Capitalize on the chaos. Divide and conquer."

"We tried that, remember?" Rachel said. "The time we pretended to help Visser One destroy Visser Three. It didn't go over real well."

"This is different," Marco replied flatly. "It's not about my mother this time. It's not personal."

Not personal? Marco didn't know how wrong he was.

"Tobias," Jake said. "I still think this should be your call." He looked up at my perch on the rafter. "Do we deal with Taylor or not?"

I looked away from the group, out through the loft window. Out at the moon, gigantic on the horizon.

People have told me that when the moon fills the sky like that, when it looms huge like a glow-in-the-dark beach ball, it's really just an illusion. It's your mind playing tricks on you. And it's true.

If you look at the moon through a camera lens, it's just a dinky dot in the sky. Our minds make it bigger than it is.

<She's dangerous,> I said after a moment, <but if we face her together . . .>

I stopped. What if Taylor was all I knew she was and worse? I looked back at the orange-white moon. I knew it was just an illusion, but I couldn't take my eyes off it, immense and amazing.

<I don't know,> I said finally. <But I think we have to deal.>

Win or lose, *I* had to deal.

CHAPTER 8

The freak and geek club. The middle of the night, deep in the forest. Four kids and a bird crowded around a laptop salvaged from a Dumpster and repaired by an alien kid and friend, Ax. An Andalite and brother of Elfangor. Ax's fourteen fingers deftly powered up the unit and dialed up the Internet.

"Ax, this is way cool," Rachel whispered, "but how did you do it? A cell phone? Internet access? That's more allowance than I'll ever see."

"You mean because Macy's has you on that pesky outfit-per-week plan?" Marco sneered.

"I'd like to think that an Andalite who once made contact with his home world could arrange Web access," Jake said.

42

<It has not been easy,> Ax said somberly. He was using an old car battery for power. All the wires and tape patches spilling from the jerry-rigged setup made Ax look pretty clever to me. <I reconditioned several other discarded computing modules and sold them to Computer Renaissance. I thought the money would be sufficient. I did not know that cell phones and Net access require a credit card.>

"The bank wasn't reassured by the whole 'unemployed alien' aspect of your application?" Marco said.

"That's right," Cassie said. "So I'm helping him. You know the cell phone I'm supposed to take with me, for emergencies only? Well, Dad made a deal with me. I can talk for half an hour a week if I do Saturday morning meds." I watched her locate the cell phone. It was opened up and tangled in a nest of wires. "Ax, you can put that back together, right?" she said, a bit nervously.

<I assure you, Cassie, I know what I am doing.> The screen dimmed and revived. Rachel raised an eyebrow. But then, sure enough, the AOL welcome screen loaded.

"Excellent," Marco said, smiling. "Oh, wait, wait! The James Bond home page! Play the teaser trailer. Ax. Listen to me!"

Ax ignored him and typed in the address to Taylor's Web page: http://www.EarthIsOurs.com.

We got a message. "The URL cannot be found."

<I do not understand. If this address existed, we would have located it,> Ax explained.

"Uh, Ax-man?" Marco pointed to the flickering screen and sounded out the address. "You typed Earth-I-saurus.com. You made it a dino. It's Earth-Is-Ours."

<Perhaps fourteen fingers are four too many.> Ax, being uncharacteristically funny. He typed in the right address.

Taylor's Web page took a while to download and the image was fuzzy at first. Slowly, the screen became clearer. It was a picture of the earth from outer space, a beautiful blue-green sphere covered with clouds. There was a caption, "Triumph will be ours," and a box to send a message.

Ax waited for my dictation. I thought about what to say. I wanted to intimidate her, cut her down to size, make her wonder if we'd bite, make her worry that we wouldn't. I wanted ambiguity. I wanted to see her squirm.

In the end, all I wrote was, "Okay, we'll play." Jake signed off with the word "Bandits." Ax clicked "send."

And then we waited. The others took turns playing minesweeper and solitaire. This time, Ax's extra fingers somehow gave him an edge.

Taylor's reply came an hour later. "No time to

lose," it read. "The plan is to attack and seize the 'Pool.' Your special skills are needed. Meet me in a public place. Let's say Borders bookstore. The wildlife section seems appropriate."

Everyone spoke at the same time.

"Seize the *Yeerk* pool?" Jake repeated.

"An attack?" Cassie.

"I'm there!" Rachel, of course.

"The wildlife section!" Marco.

<The computer has, as you say, crashed,> Ax announced coolly.

"We'll need a human morph that won't give us away," Marco echoed. "It ain't gonna be Ax. He attracts too many girls. And of course I can't go. Same reason."

"Guys," I said, half-scared, half-thrilled by the meaning of my words, "I just happen to have the perfect morph."

Six hours later, when its doors opened, I strolled into Borders bookshop. Strode past piles of self-help books and tiers of best-sellers. Despite Rachel's objections and Marco's security concerns, Jake had let me go. I needed to be the one to deal with Taylor. Jake knew that.

But even Jake had some reservations about this morph. About the victim becoming the victimizer. So for a variety of security reasons, watching from various stations both in and outside the store, were my friends.

45

Two seagulls on the roof, Ax and Cassie, watching the front door and the sky. A fluffy cat, prowling the back alley, keeping an eye on the back door. In the magazine section, a short kid with pants as wide as a tent, huge bug-eyed sunglasses, headphones, and a knit ski cap disguising nine-tenths of his face. And in a stall in the men's room, waiting for a signal, Jake, ready to provide immediate firepower if necessary.

Rachel chose the outfit, so I was dressed to kill. And I would have looked great in rags. See, morphing uses DNA, and I'd morphed her body as it would have been before the fire, before the accident. No artificial arm. No reconstructed beauty.

I was a cover girl who could give even Angelina Jolie a run for her money. I was . . .

"Taylor," I said easily, coming up behind the tall blond wandering the wildlife section. She spun around, surprised and off guard. Her mouth dropped open. She was face-to-face with herself. And for a second, I'd trumped her. She was mine.

"That's clever," she conceded, recovering quickly like a good detached Yeerk should. "Yeah, a nice touch. But how? Is there some new, improved Andalite morphing technology that allows you to acquire while in morph?"

I smiled on the outside. On the inside, I

46

seized up. I'd just given myself away. But she'd never figure it out. Would she? She'd never know the whole story, that my true form was hawk, that I was no Andalite. But already, I'd given her more than I'd wanted to.

I searched the brain of my new body for a savvy reply. A strategic comeback. I searched it for the ruthless, crushing Yeerk. What I found was gentleness, fear, and joy. Very little cunning. Almost no hate. The human Taylor had once been an average kid. Like me. Like I'd been.

The realization steeled me against the nervousness that gnawed at my stomach.

"You're not the only ones with scientists," I said guardedly.

She accepted that answer. We walked toward the cafe.

CHAPTER 9

The high school kid behind the counter stared wide-eyed. One, make that two very attractive girls were closing in on him.

"Uh, what can I get you?" he asked shakily.

"Decaf latte with skim," Taylor purred.

The kid turned to take my order. I smiled and he almost fell over. It was crazy to have such power. I'd been on the receiving end before. I'd just never been the source. Is this what Rachel experienced? Was this part of what made her so brave?

"Triple espresso. Heavy on the cream and the sugar."

Taylor turned to me. "You dare abuse my body, you filthy grass eater?"

The kid raised his eyebrows. "Grass?" he said. "I can juice you some wheat grass, but that's all we have."

Taylor glared at the boy. I laughed. We were mirror images, literal carbon copies. But I was alive. Taylor wasn't. Not really. I had a sense of humor. Taylor had a coldness that enclosed her like a shield. The kid could see this. Anybody could.

We brought our drinks to a table and sat in opposing chairs. Three college kids were studying together nearby, but out of earshot. A writer was reading her work to an enraptured public thirty feet away. Salsa music spilled out of the speakers.

Taylor gripped her mug like it was the enemy.

"I suppose you want details," she said icily.

"Of course."

"Listen carefully," she began, her voice hushed. "There's a natural gas pipeline, a large one, that runs a half mile from the Yeerk pool. We need to dig a connecting tunnel from that pipeline to the pool."

"Why?"

Taylor huffed, arrogant and exasperated. "So that the pipe can be ruptured. So that thousands of tons of natural gas will spew into the Yeerk pool complex. And so that the gas, when exploded, will kill everyone exposed. The hosts. The Yeerks."

49

It was a disgusting plan. It was even more horrible than I expected.

I took a sip of coffee, to keep it looking natural. Twin teens, probably comparing notes on last night's dates. "That's what you call a giant leap for democracy? I don't get it. You want to end the violence with a big bang of your own? You think the violence will end there?"

"Surely you see that we need a bargaining chip," Taylor replied. "We have to take control of the place and oust Visser Three. We have to get some leverage. Without this plan — if the rebels tried a more peaceful protest — the Yeerks in orbit would oppose us. But if the plan works, we have a Yeerk pool full of hostages. They couldn't attack us without putting their own at risk."

"That never stopped you Yeerks before," I retorted.

"Well, the Yeerks in orbit have to feed, don't they?" she shot back angrily. "There's no way around that. Within three days every Yeerk will need Kandrona rays. They will be forced to accept rebel leadership. If they want to survive."

I forced a false tone of admiration. A little flattery wouldn't hurt with this egomaniacal Yeerk. "This plan is your brainchild, isn't it? It's brutal, ruthless. Brilliant, really."

"You know me well, Andalite." A smile washed over her face.

But then, suddenly, her face transformed. All at once, her blue eyes filled with desperation. Her pink lips parted in wordless horror. A different voice, a frightened, abused little voice, called across the table in a toneless whisper.

"Don't listen," it said. "Don't listen to her!"

I sat transfixed as Taylor's hand blazed across the tabletop, crashing into her latte, smashing the mug to the floor. There was a huge racket as ceramic clattered across tile.

The writer stopped her public reading. The students raised their heads. The salsa music trumpeted on.

"Miss, are you okay?" The high school kid was instantly at Taylor's side. She was crouched on the floor, her head in her arms. A second passed. Two seconds. Silence. On the third, her head snapped up.

"I'm fine," she said, climbing back into her chair. "Get me a refill." Her face was strong again, controlled. And I knew what I'd just seen.

Taylor the Yeerk had a rigid command over her host body. No longer did she let her human speak independently. No. Somehow, she'd severed their collaboration. Except they'd been partners for so long, the host could still break in, on occasion. Taylor the girl could still break in. Did break in . . .

Why? Why would the Yeerk wait until this moment to fully enslave her host? She claimed to be interested in democracy and peace. It didn't compute.

"Any questions?" Taylor inquired, as if nothing had happened. As if the conversation hadn't been disrupted by a distinctly Yeerk version of multiple personality disorder.

"Yeah," I said. "First one. A natural gas explosion as large as the one you're planning will collapse the Yeerk pool. And the city built above it. It will devastate everything for miles."

"My allies are in control of the pumping station," Taylor answered calmly. "The amount of gas will be carefully controlled. The Yeerk pool will not collapse."

"Fine. Question two. Just how do you plan to tunnel through the earth, from the pipeline to the pool?"

"I don't. That's where you come in."

"That's absurd," I laughed. "No earth animal, no morph we Andalites have, could do that kind of job in less than weeks. And even then, it would just be a tiny tunnel. Not nearly enough to move the volume of gas you're talking about."

"That's why I selected an animal for you to morph that can do the job in hours, not days or weeks." Her lips curled into a devilish smile. "You always underestimate me, Andalite."

"What morph?" I asked. She wrapped the fingers of her artificial hand around my arm and started to squeeze.

"I have a morph that will leave behind a tunnel at least as large in circumference as the pipe itself."

"What morph?" I repeated.

"Taxxon, my Andalite friend. Taxxon!"

CHAPTER 10

"Is she insane?" Marco cried. He'd ditched the ski cap and sunglasses but the headphones still hung around his neck.

"Yes. I believe we established that during our last encounter." Ax, of course. He'd gone from seagull to Andalite to eerily attractive human boy in a Dumpster conveniently located behind the bookstore.

"Taxxon! I'd rather morph E. coli. I'd rather morph an ant again."

"That's kind of what Taxxons are like, isn't it?" Jake said. "Brainless, driven, starved."

"Who knows?" Rachel shrugged impatiently. In the time between demorphing from cat and joining the rest of us, Rachel had slipped into

The Gap and bought a couple of T-shirts. No moss grows on that girl. "But I can handle it. I'm in."

"Whoa." Cassie held up an arm. "Wait a minute. Who says we're even gonna do this?"

I'd demorphed in the Borders bathroom. Jake had left a bag of clothing behind a trash container. I remorphed as my human self, and crossed the street to the mall. Now I sat in the food court listening to my friends freak out.

"When do we have to give her an answer?" Jake asked me.

"We don't. We just show up at the natural gas pumping facility tonight. Or we don't."

"Answer me this," Marco said, rolling a plastic straw between his palms. "If Taxxons are all Controllers, why doesn't She-Yeerk just ask a fellow Controller with a Taxxon host to do the digging?"

I explained. "She says Yeerks are only ever partly in control of their Taxxon hosts. It's impossible to master the Taxxon hunger, the murderous tendencies, the cannibalistic urges. Taxxon hosts are given only to low-ranking Yeerks and, big surprise, soon they're more Taxxon than Yeerk."

"But I've seen them take orders. I've watched Taxxons move on command," Marco persisted. "They fly Bug fighters for . . ."

"Right. But no one would ever trust a Taxxon to be part of a conspiracy. You can't count on a

55

guy who'll sell out for a chunk of rotting meat. Most of her allies are human-Controllers, anyway," I added.

Ax broke in. "I was once told that controlling a Taxxon morph is like facing the ultimate temptation. Tay-shun. The more you resist the temptation, the stronger it becomes, until it ends by carrying you so far beyond the realm of conscious, controllable thought you become lost in the Taxxon's most basic instincts."

"Well then, what am I waiting for?" Marco said sarcastically. "Sign me up! An army of cold, power-hungry Yeerks can't control the Taxxons. Not to worry. The short kid who got a B-minus in gym won't have any problems."

Rachel smirked. "You got a B-minus in *gym?*"

Marco rolled his eyes and looked exasperated. "People, if the Yeerks can't control a Taxxon, how in the world can we?"

"Taylor says we'd only stay morphed for short periods," I said, feeling like her press secretary. Like part of her team. It was definitely weird. "And we'd morph one at a time, surrounded by enough force to control any out-of-control behavior."

Jake frowned. Marco looked skeptical. Cassie's eyes were darkening with some serious issues.

We all needed to think. Ax wanted to eat. So, Marco and Jake volunteered to get food.

Cassie, Rachel, and Ax sat silently. I looked around. It was Friday, so the food court was crowded. Packed with a bunch of normal people, leading normal lives. Ordinary, mundane, wonderful lives. All these normal people — moms and dads, kids and grandparents — represented the very thing we were fighting for. Humanity.

Marco returned and set nachos for me and Ax on the table. I wasn't very hungry. I wasn't used to eating with others around and there were people everywhere. Very different from my life as a hawk. When you're a hawk, you get nervous when you can't feed in peace. Someone could swoop in and steal your dinner. Or someone could swoop in and eat you.

Jake reappeared and placed a large plastic tray piled with two hamburgers, three fries, a veggie wrap, and three large plastic cups on the table.

"Cassie, veggie wrap and orange soda," he said, handing her one of the cups and the sandwich. "7-up, Rachel. Coke, me. So," he added, sitting, "where are we?"

"Seems clear enough to me," Rachel said with a mouth half-stuffed with hamburger. "Destroying the Yeerk pool can only be a good thing.

It's the chance we've been waiting for. It could be the beginning of the end." She paused and swallowed. "Let's fry some Yeerk butt."

"I agree with Rachel," Ax said, looking up from the plastic Radio Shack bag he was rummaging through and reaching for a tub of nachos. "Strategically speaking, this is a very interesting opportunity. Even in spite of the risk."

Jake looked up at me with an encouraging nod.

"Just remember, she can't be trusted," I reminded everyone. "She . . ." I paused. The others were looking at me like they were being extra careful to be polite. Just like at the barn, they were waiting for me to finish. No interruptions. No snide remarks.

The Borders meeting should have proved to them that I was over the fear! I'd handled it fine. I wasn't the one who'd broken down.

I tried to sound extra calm and sure of myself so they would stop worrying, stop doubting. "Even if she doesn't have it in for us, our work is only going to make her more power hungry. You can count on it. It's not like she's suddenly had a change of heart. That democracy stuff has got to be BS."

"Absolutely," Marco said. "A free Yeerk society? Give me a break. Let's just imagine the scenario for a second. Everyone in favor of having his free will replaced by a slimy, stinking slug that will take over his brain, say, 'yea.' Those opposed say, 'nay.'"

"Okay," Jake interrupted. "We get it. We all admit that Taylor can't be trusted. Marco and Tobias saw her lose it at Borders. She's obviously got some problems. But even given the weirdness, I think we agree this could be one of the most important missions we've had."

CHAPTER 11

No one said anything. Silent agreement. Except for Cassie.

Her eyes got wide. She began to stand up.

"None of you guys are really thinking about this," she said in a voice that made a couple of older kids sitting at the table next to ours look up.

"Shhh."

"No," she said. "It's wrong. I won't. I don't want to judge you guys, but you're talking about strategy and risk like this is some computer game. Like there aren't others involved. Have you forgotten that we're supposed to be in this to save lives?"

Jake put his hand on her shoulder and gently

encouraged her to sit back down. No one seemed to know what to say. She continued. She spoke very quietly, but urgently.

"Has anyone stopped to think that we'll be responsible for the death of hundreds, maybe thousands of people? People who already suffer the worst fate imaginable? And not that any of you care, but we'll be killing thousands of defenseless Yeerks right along with them."

"My God, you mean we'd be killing Yeerks?" Marco said with a straight face. "That's . . . that's unthinkable!"

No one laughed.

"Let her finish," Rachel whispered.

"They're not all like Visser Three," Cassie went on. "We know that. Some of the Yeerks and Controllers are just kids like us. They never had a choice. They participate or they're eliminated. And it's not like they get the information they need to make an informed decision. If you'd been raised since birth on empire propaganda, you'd fight to take over Earth, too."

"You make an interesting argument," Ax said through a mouthful of nachos. "But there are a lot of inconsistencies between what you say and what you do." He swallowed noisily. "How can you make this argument knowing what you've done in the past?"

"That's different," Cassie responded forcefully. "I'm not against defending myself and you guys. I hate violence, but self-defense is justified, in all societies. Unlike murdering people . . ."

"Killing slugs," Marco corrected.

"Killing Yeerks when they're defenseless, when they're not engaged in battle, when they're not actively threatening our lives . . . no! You don't . . . why can't you . . . can't you see!" She stopped. I could almost feel the passion radiating from her body. "It's . . . it's just not right."

"But they *are* threatening our lives," Rachel insisted. "Not just ours, everyone's. Just by being who they are."

"Yeah, and why do you think they're at the Yeerk pool?" Marco put in. "I can tell you this much. It's not because they're planning Earth Day activities.

"Look, during World War Two we bombed factories and highways and railroads. Even regular cities. Just because someone's not wearing a uniform or carrying a weapon doesn't mean they're not fighting a war. I know this plan is bad, Cassie, but we've gotta think of the big picture." He looked at her and touched her shoulder again.

"Yes," Ax said calmly. "The Yeerk pool is a command and control center. It is central to

Yeerk military activity. They recharge there so they can continue their conquest."

"Not true," Cassie insisted, regaining her voice. She leaned forward. "What about Tidwell, and others like him in the peace movement? They have to go to the pool because they'll die if they don't feed. For them, it's no different than eating."

"The peace movement Yeerks are a small minority," Jake countered coldly. "We can't really consider them, except maybe to warn them."

"Not consider them!" Cassie repeated disbelievingly. "What if your brother's at the pool when the gas explodes?"

Jake looked at his hands. "I guess it's a sacrifice I have to deal with in order to protect thousands more," Jake said, his voice now expressionless.

"Jake, I don't believe you!"

"You should," he said, looking back to Cassie. To me. "Besides, family involvement doesn't really come into play here. It can't. The Yeerk pool is a target. End of discussion. It's not like we're bombing a bunch of innocent people at the mall on a Friday afternoon . . ."

Again, I looked at the people all around us. Families, couples, kids like us. Enjoying themselves. Here to see a movie, meet their friends, shop for clothes. They'd done the jobs they had to do at work or at school. Now was their chance to relax. Have fun.

Cassie looked around the food court, too, and then back at Jake.

"Isn't it?"

CHAPTER 12

That's pretty much when Cassie decided she couldn't do it. She decided to sit the mission out. I admired her. I even thought about pulling out myself.

But who would be around to figure out Taylor? Who would be there to watch for sabotage? I'm not really sure how or why we decided I was the best one for the job. But I decided to do it.

Early that evening Ax and I flew together, an owl and a red-tailed hawk, high up into the night sky so we could get a good look at the place before we landed. We wanted to be as sure as possible that we weren't flying into a trap. The natural gas pumping station came into view.

<The coast appears to be clear,> Ax relayed. <Why do humans refer to the "coast" when talking about a precarious situation?>

<I don't know,> I said. <It's just what we say.>

There wasn't anything within a half mile of the structure. Just trees and bushes. I swooped low to check out an abandoned van left a few hundred feet from the pumping station. No hidden group of Hork-Bajir waiting for us.

The pumping station was pretty small, just a square building almost as big as a house. Security lights brightened it like a baseball stadium just before a night game. The lights made my hawk vision work almost as well as the owl's. Through the few windows, I could see a maze of pipes.

We landed on the ground behind a line of heavy brush. It's hard to land directly on the ground. It's easier when you can grab on to something with your talons. I skidded a little. Ax was right behind me.

<Well, Ax-man, I guess it's now or never — and, boy, do I wish it was never,> I said.

I morphed and Ax demorphed. Two identical blue aliens began to sprout from the bushes. I like the way Andalite morph feels. It's about strength and agility. A focused yet playful mind.

An unwavering optimism that's invaluable when you're up against pure evil.

We finished morphing and Ax trotted up beside me. His main eyes studied me. His stalk eyes scanned the area around us. Then, suddenly, his tail snapped and zipped across the blue-and-tan fur on my chest.

<Hey, watch it! What are you doing?>

<I am removing portions of your fur. We call it *"unschweet."* I believe you say haircut. I must make you look less like my genetic double.>

<Fine,> I said. <But be careful. No razor burn.>

<When an Andalite warrior is reprimanded for his conduct,> Ax continued, <a superior officer removes some of the offender's fur so that the transgression is not soon forgotten. In the ritual of *unschweet,* the wrongdoer is not punished in the traditional sense. He must live with the constant reminder of his error, and the scrutiny of his peers. As his fur grows back, he is slowly redeemed until, finally, the incident is laid to rest and the warrior is whole again.>

<I've had bad haircuts before but I never knew what to call them. So Ax, do I deserve *unschweet?*>

<No,> Ax answered. <But it is the only way I know to cut fur. Sorry.>

<It's cool. Let's just get this over with.>

We walked cautiously toward the pumping station, staying out of the brightest lights and watching our backs with our stalk eyes. A tall cyclone fence topped with barbed wire ran all around the structure, but the rear gate was open a crack. Someone was expecting us.

I pointed a slender finger toward the gate.

Ax moved out in front. An eerie squeak cut the still air as we slipped through the gate.

We moved quickly toward the shadows that clung to the wall of the building.

"Evening, boys."

She stepped out of nowhere. A dark, human form with a voice that sent chills down my spine.

It was Taylor.

"Nice to see you. I've been waiting."

She'd been there the whole time. I couldn't believe it. We'd been so careful. How had we missed her?

She was wearing dark leather from head to toe. Tall boots that came up to her knees. Her long blond hair was tucked into a high leather collar. It was a new look. Good-bye preppy. Hello soldier. We stared.

"I'm not here to be gawked at. I'm here to deliver a present," she sneered. "I know how much you both like Taxxons. I found a choice one —

very big, very mean — to show my appreciation for your help. Follow me."

She disappeared into the pumping station. Ax followed her. I followed Ax.

We had to duck low to clear some of the pipes. The noise was unbearable, a constant clanging that made my head hurt. Taylor descended a twisting metal ramp into the basement. We followed, stepping carefully on the slick surface.

Downstairs it was considerably darker, though there were fewer pipes. Taylor stopped in a corner of the room and gestured to an iron handle protruding from the smooth concrete floor. Then she backed up, leaned against the wall, and crossed her arms over her chest.

"He's in there."

Ax and I looked more carefully. The iron handle was attached to a large slab of concrete set into the floor.

<This is it,> I said to Ax. Trying to forget I was in the same room with the monster who'd come close to destroying what little peace of mind I'd ever had. I bent down and grabbed the iron handle with my relatively weak Andalite arm. It didn't budge.

<I will assist you,> Ax announced. Together we pulled with all our strength. The slab rose out of the floor. With great effort, we set it to one

side. A snort from below sent us both jumping back.

"How cute," Taylor said. "You're scared."

<We are not frightened,> Ax said coldly. <We are cautious.> He stepped up to the hole and peered inside. <I see no sign of the Taxxon.>

Taylor tilted her head to one side and looked at Ax mockingly. "Then go get him, silly."

CHAPTER 13

The cavern was dark. I could just make out the bottom, about ten feet away. It seemed to curve slightly. I guessed it was a tank, an old fuel storage reservoir or something.

The last thing I wanted to do was jump into a dark tank with a Taxxon waiting to eat me.

Again, Ax led the way. If he wasn't fearless, he was putting on a good show.

<It is a long way down, Tobias,> he called from below. <Bend your knees on impact.>

Taylor was watching, her beautiful face wearing the look of perpetual disdain she'd perfected. I couldn't let her see my fear. I hopped over the edge and braced for impact.

WHAAAMMM!

71

My hooves hit hard on the concrete bottom. Damp darkness enveloped me. I could just make out Ax at my side.

<Where is he?> I asked. <What if there's no Taxxon at all? What if it's a trap?> I thought of the others waiting outside, hidden in various morphs, watching. They were ready to storm the place if we got into trouble. But how long would it take them to reach us? I looked up and imagined being sealed in the tank. But then I remembered that Taylor couldn't lift the cover alone.

Or could she? How strong was that artificial arm?

It didn't matter. No. Between the two of us, Ax and I could probably come up with a few morphs that would get us out. But that comforting thought came too late to stop my hearts from racing. We stared into darkness, searching for the Taxxon.

Before he found us.

Ax moved forward and disappeared. I strained to catch sight of him in the blackness. I saw slight movement to my right.

<Is that you, Ax?> I reached out to make sure of where he stood and . . .

<Ahhhhhhh!>

Agony shot up my arm.

<Ax!>

The Taxxon bit down hard. A thousand razor

teeth shredded my flesh and muscle. He didn't sever my arm and have a quick snack. No. He sucked with iron jaws. Pulling me in. Dragging me closer to his stomach.

I swung my tail blade, but lost my balance on the smooth, curved floor. My hooves skidded wildly as the vile mouth chewed. I was caught in a slow-motion wood chipper!

Glowing red eyes, inching toward me . . .

I whipped my tail blade frantically, slashing the blackness, missing the Taxxon. The force of his jaws would rip off my arm!

<Ax!>

FWAP!

Razor teeth withdrew and I stumbled back, clutching my mutilated arm. I looked up. Dizzy. Ill.

<Hurry,> Ax said. <We must move quickly. I fear I have mortally wounded the Taxxon.>

Stupefying pain throbbed in what was left of my arm. I backed away. I could feel a wet, sticky ooze beneath my hooves. The Taxxon's vital fluids were spilling across the bottom of the tank.

I bent down. Reached out my good hand and touched the Taxxon's side. His soft side heaved laboriously, up and down, as he struggled to breathe. Yes, he was dying.

I could see Ax in the faint light, already acquiring him. I began to demorph. When the transition was complete, I reached out a talon and placed it on the disgusting flesh.

I could feel life draining from his body, and the firm folds of bloated tissue collapsing like a torn hot air balloon. I concentrated on the acquisition.

Usually, you don't feel anything about an animal while you acquire it. This time, I sensed something. Fierce and elemental, like a scream of rage.

I finished acquiring the Taxxon's DNA. And realized there was something inside me unlike anything I had ever known.

Maybe it was just my own tormented mind at work. Or maybe it really was the DNA, screaming at me on some microscopic level. It was something terrible.

Something dangerous.

A tortured shudder moved the length of the Taxxon's body, from head to tail and back again. He shook for one violent instant, then stopped.

And I realized that he now lived only in Ax and me.

CHAPTER 14

<It's sure enough about time, Bird-boy.> Marco's thought-speak greeted me at about three hundred feet. He was flying in, too, and was just as late as I was. It was dawn. We were both working hard to stay up in the cool air.

<Enjoying a leisurely breakfast while the rest of us get ready to work?> he continued.

Actually, breakfast was why I was late. This morning, the meadow had been unusually still. Not a field mouse anywhere. Kind of ominous, like they knew something I didn't. Like they knew it was better to stay at home.

I'd set out hungry, but along the way I'd spotted a gray squirrel. It was bigger than I like, but food is all I think about. In nature, in my world, hunger doesn't just mean you'll be crabby in the car on the way to Taco Bell. It carries undertones of death.

I'd dived, silent and swift. With wide-open talons I snatched it, unsuspecting, from the power line it was making its way across. The squirrel was heavier than I'd guessed. It yanked on my legs, sent me tumbling for the ground. I held tight. I even regained control, feet above the ground, flapping like mad to stay aloft.

But then, the squirrel's teeth pierced my leg. Sharp pain from the incision shot to my brain. I released one talon and let go of my would-be breakfast.

<Some of us actually have to work for our food,> I called to Marco. <But then, it's probably a huge deal for you to get the Pop-Tart in the toaster.>

I landed gently on a tree branch. Marco was already demorphing. The others had gathered a few feet away. All but Ax, who was hiding in the thick grass, keeping an eye on the pumping station.

Jake had changed plans on Taylor at the last minute. He had to balance the danger of not having her accounted for as we dug with the risk of having our true identities discovered when we demorphed.

So Jake had let Taylor know, by E-mail, that

76

she couldn't come within a mile of the dig or the pumping station before 8:00 A.M. If she did, the deal was off. When she did show up, she had to hang with us as we dug.

She had agreed to Jake's conditions with an eagerness I found disconcerting. I didn't mention it to the others. I knew it was nerves.

I could see the manhole cover next to where the others were standing. It was partly covered with sand and stuck out above the ground a few inches. This was a good place to work, with little chance of being seen. We weren't far from the pumping station but were concealed by trees and brush on all sides. Taylor knew what she was doing.

The sewer cap was in a cul-de-sac, on the side of a gravel road that hadn't been paved. The concrete curbs were in place and the gravel was carefully compacted a few inches below, ready for a layer of asphalt. It had been this way for a while. The site was supposed to be a new industrial park. But local residents didn't want the noise and the traffic, so construction had been temporarily stopped, leaving sewers and electricity, but little else.

"Your left talon's bleeding," Rachel said.

I didn't answer at first. I didn't feel like explaining. But Rachel's concern was genuine. It wasn't fair to blow her off.

<Breakfast sometimes bites back,> I answered.

"You're telling me," Marco broke in. "I was looking in the toaster to see if my Pop-Tart was done and wham, the thing shot out and hit me in the eye."

<I'll be fine,> I said, looking Rachel's way.

"Let me have a look," Cassie said. She was still adamant about not going on this mission, but she wanted to know where we were digging.

In case we didn't come back.

Cassie's being there was a little awkward. Maybe least so for me, I don't know. She wasn't there to wish us luck. And although Jake always gives us the option, it's really rare that one of us decides not to fight.

"You should morph to fix the cut," Jake said. "That thing's going to get infected. So I guess you'll go first."

I'd go first? That slammed me into the reality I'd been trying to avoid. I wasn't looking forward to the work that lay ahead. Or to the creature I had to become.

<The time is now 7:50.> Ax came trotting out of the bushes and stopped next to Jake. <The pumping station is clear, Prince Jake. We should start digging.>

Ax was wearing a Timex Triathlon timepiece around his front ankle. Rachel had picked it out for him. He feared that his internal clock might be thrown off by the power of the Taxxon morph. He and I were going to take turns wearing it while Andalite.

He moved briskly to the manhole cover, stuck the tip of his tail blade in the small hole intended for the crowbar and, with one swift, fluid twist of his tail, sent the fifty-pound steel cap tumbling through the air. It landed with dull resonance inches from Jake's feet.

"Smooth," Jake commented dryly. "You should work for the city."

I dropped from my perch to the edge of the hole. I could see that at the bottom of an eight-foot shaft was a cylindrical chamber.

<I think I'll morph when I get down there,> I said. <Wouldn't want to be responsible for any-one spewing their breakfast.>

I hopped over the edge of the hole into the darkness, falling slowly, with partially open wings. A real hawk would never drop into such a tight space. I could feel the raptor's anxiety. I landed softly on the surface of the curved concrete.

"Take it easy, Tobias," Jake encouraged. "Nice and steady. If you have problems, we're here."

<Remember that you may not be able to control it like other morphs,> Ax instructed. <It might be too overwhelming to suppress. The few Andalites who have successfully used the Taxxon

morph speak of becoming one with the animal's nature, of channeling the violent energy. It cannot be stopped. But you can try to direct it. Use it, do not try to overcome it.>

"I'm right here, Tobias," Rachel called.

"Be careful." Cassie. "And . . . I'll see you guys later."

"Tobias . . ." Jake began.

<I can handle it, you guys,> I said, assuring myself as much as my friends. <I'll be okay.>

CHAPTER 15

I closed my eyes and focused on the DNA I carried within me.

The changes started immediately. Continued concentration wasn't necessary. Once it began, the morph gained momentum on its own, like a rock dislodged from a hilltop.

Hissssssss . . .

I felt my bones disintegrating. No, melting. All the hard parts of my body — talons, beak, feather shafts — softened and liquefied. Usually when you morph, you feel the firm shape of new organs forming. This morph was exactly the opposite. Everything was dissolving, then congealing into one hideous continuum.

I fell down on the cement as my legs melted

away, only to be lifted up again as hundreds of cone-shaped appendages shot out of a soft, rapidly extending belly.

I was taking on the shape of a worm. Long and formless.

Crystal-clear hawk vision blurred. Think about driving into the rain without turning on the windshield wipers. Then this murky vision was traded for —

Whoa! A thousand tiny fragments of my surroundings. Visual shards, like a kaleidoscope image with blurred edges.

I knew that Taxxons had compound eyes, like flies. Each red eye is really a thousand smaller eyes, each scanning a small piece of the world. What I hadn't known was that Taxxon brains aren't quite sophisticated enough to put all the pieces together.

The mouth formed last. The center of the Taxxon's existence.

The changes stopped.

Then, all at once, I felt it coming. An unstoppable tidal wave riding up the shore.

Insane, insane hunger.

Desperate, all-consuming hunger. Like nothing you can begin to imagine. It reared up, larger than any urge I had ever experienced. Blocking out everything else.

Everything.

I could smell the others. Up aboveground. I knew exactly where they stood. I heard vibrations. Their feet through the soil.

I was over ten feet long. Long enough to crawl up and squirm through the hole. I pictured Marco. And the next thing I knew I imagined him in my mouth, his soft tan flesh, sawed up. Swallowed. And Jake. Bigger. And Ax . . .

My worm body lunged for the hole. Before I could stop it. Before I could think. I didn't know what was happening. The smell was so strong. The imagined taste so real. The Taxxon mind so in need!

Noxious digestive acid poured from my mouth. My soft head pushed against the iron cover Marco and Jake had put partially back in place.

I would devour them. Lunge and devour.

Marco and Jake and Ax and . . .

Rachel.

My Taxxon body twitched. The thought of even more food excited it. But something . . . something way in the back of my mind, way deep in there, spoke out.

Rachel?

I stopped. I heard something. The tiny, in-significant voice of a kid. Tobias, the human in me, was struggling to make his presence known. Somewhere beneath the Taxxon's evil and unimaginable power, the kid in me was ranting like a lunatic. *Stop,* he cried. *Stop! Stop! Stop!*

I can't say that I regained control. That would be a lie. Like saying that the captain of a sailboat can take control of a storm.

But somehow I steered the enormous beast away from the other Animorphs. Somehow.

It was impossible to stop the hunger, impossible to slow it down, but Ax had told me I could focus it on something else. Okay. I turned it to the job at hand.

We had heard that the Taxxon was a great digger. But that's not true. Not exactly. The Taxxon is great at one thing. Eating.

Suddenly, ravenously, I began to devour the dirt beside the hole Taylor's people had jackhammered in the concrete pipe. I turned the full force of the Taxxon's hunger on the dirt.

I was inhaling soil like I hadn't eaten in forty days. I bit off large chunks, coated them with digestive enzymes, and swallowed the sticky gobs. Bite after bite. After bite after bite. The Taxxon was insatiable.

In no time at all I had excavated a body-sized chamber. Dirt walls grew up around me as I lunged and gobbled and swallowed and secreted.

That's right. Secreted. I was scarfing down pounds per second. I was the dump truck hauling away the excavated dirt. I was an all-in-one machine. Earthmover, waste disposal system. And that waste, that soil by-product, passed out of my Taxxon body as a thick, sludgy layer. A goo, that coated all surfaces of the tunnel that began to develop as I tried desperately to satisfy an unsatisfiable hunger.

"Tobias? Ugh! Man, what's that stench?" Jake's voice reached me as a weak distraction, a vague disturbance. "Tobias, are you okay down there?"

I ignored him. I just kept eating. Or digging. Just like an earthworm, passing dirt right through my system to extract the organic material. Except that unlike an earthworm, I had a ring of razor teeth to speed things up. Multiply an earthworm's speed and size by about a million and you begin to get the picture.

Except that with a Taxxon, there's no hope of satisfying the hunger with dirt, not even momentarily. There aren't enough nutrients in the soil. Just enough to smell, to trigger the urge to eat. Just enough to keep me wanting more.

"Look at him move!" It was Marco's voice. They were nearer now. They must have dropped into the sewer. "He can't get no . . ." Marco gasped, probably from the stink of my secretion. "Satisfaction." He gasped again.

The longer I dug, the hungrier and more frantic I got. I didn't learn until later that a Taxxon will dig, starved and exhausted, until he dies.

<Tobias,> Rachel called in thought-speak. She had already morphed. The others must be right behind her. <Answer us. Say something.>

<More!>

CHAPTER 16

<Tobias, time's up, man. Take a break. Demorph.>

Jake.

The reminder of human flesh was more than I could resist.

I sped backward, sloshing through the goo, racing toward the others. I flew out of the hole into the underground area. A slithering worm. Massive, starved, desperate.

<Whoa,> Jake cautioned.

<Whoahh!> Marco agreed.

My compound eyes filled with the broken blue form of an Andalite, the hulking masses of a gorilla and a grizzly bear, the sharp stripes of a tiger.

No pink flesh! No soft pink flesh!

I'd make do.

The Andalite was nearest. I smelled the flesh under his fur, the muscles under his flesh. I was aware of his tail blade. It even triggered a danger alarm in the Taxxon mind. But the siren was faint, nearly insignificant. The tail blade could slash me in two, but I didn't care. I might get a bite in first!

<Watch yourself, Ax-man!> Jake called. <He's coming at you. Tobias! Get a grip on the morph. Get a grip!>

I rushed full speed at Ax. I'd body-slam him. Knock him to the ground. Lock my teeth in his skin and eat him whole!

But then I saw something else. Something that made even the Taxxon stop. My legs froze.

Taylor. Dressed in a tank top and soft, thin, cotton khakis.

Her clothes would melt in my mouth. Her soft pink shoulders beckoned to be devoured.

I heaved my bulk in her direction. Began to move toward her. Crawling. Slinking.

"Just try, worm," she hissed, aiming a Dracon beam at my head, "and I'll fry you on setting six."

<You gave us your word, Yeerk,> Ax objected, edging toward her. <You promised not to use a setting higher than three.>

"Did I?" Taylor laughed. "Then try and stop

me." She turned back to me. "I'd love to have an excuse to finish you off." Her voice wavered slightly, almost nervously. I continued inching toward her. "But then, if you're the coward I know, you'd rather be stuck as a Taxxon *nothlit* than die with courage."

My Taxxon hunger fused with human hatred. I realized how much easier it would be to eat her than to fight the urge. How much easier it would be even to die than to face Yeerk-girl. This monster who haunted me day and night. With contempt. Arrogance. Power over me!

Had it been like this at the Yeerk pool? Deep beneath the murderous hunger, my mind wondered. Had I overstayed the two-hour time limit so I wouldn't have to face simple facts of life? Being a boy, living with foster parents, school, Rachel, Taylor . . .

Marco grabbed me gently, attempting to stop me. I hissed and shook him off.

<Tobias,> Rachel called. <Stop. Just stop!> But she didn't block my path.

Was I a coward?

In the wild, there's only life or death. You feed your belly or you die. Success is survival. Failure is death. It's simple. There's no middle ground. At least, not for very long.

Was I a coward?

I hated Taylor.

Because she knew the answer to that question.

Because she saw weakness in me. She saw it because she was weak herself. People recognize their own kind. She'd sold out to save face. Literally. She'd become a voluntary Controller and betrayed her own mother because she wanted to be pretty again.

It was beyond sad. It was pathetic.

Was I different, or was I just like her?

I'd trapped myself. Why?

I hated Taylor because she knew.

I was going to destroy her.

I rushed forward. Opened my mouth. Scrambled for her legs.

Tseew!

A bolt of Dracon fire knocked me down. Not strong enough to kill, but tough enough to paralyze the Taxxon body and keep me down long enough to regain control. And begin to demorph.

I focused hard. The bloated worm began to disappear. I imagined the first signs of my familiar hawk body emerging from the pool of Taxxon slime. And then I remembered . . .

Taylor was watching this! She couldn't see me go from Taxxon to bird. She couldn't know I was a *nothlit*. She thought I was Andalite. A mighty Andalite.

I'd already slipped once, at Borders. Not again.

I focused harder and tried to do something that can't really be done. Morph directly from Taxxon to Andalite. The instant my hawk parts emerged, I focused on remorphing them to Andalite. It was excruciating, exhausting. Probably not very convincing.

Was she looking? Could she tell? Would she see what she shouldn't see?

The others were smart. Smarter than I was. Rachel and Marco had backed Taylor against a wall, blocking her view with their gigantic bodies. As I demorphed and remorphed, Jake kept guard and talked.

<I said you could carry a Dracon beam for protection,> Jake said firmly. <But we had an agreement. You would not fire above setting three.>

"Yeah, well, it didn't even work. What's wrong with this beam?"

<You're one lucky worm,> Jake said to me privately. <Ax saved your butt. He modified her weapon so it wouldn't fire beyond setting three.>

<She lied,> Rachel said coldly in private thought-speak. <Strike one. She'd have fried you if she could, Tobias. You'd be a smoldering pile of slime if she'd had her way. I say we end this right here. She can't keep a deal.>

91

<Wait,> I said, finishing the morph to Andalite. <I'm fine. I'm okay. Maybe she knew you'd tampered with the Dracon. Maybe she was just playing it up to scare me.>

<She did not know,> Ax said as Taylor threw the Dracon beam to the floor. He moved behind Jake to give my Andalite fur a quick tail-blade trim.

<Well, I was about to take a bite out of her. She acted in self-defense.>

<She knows that's why we're here,> Marco answered angrily. <To keep you under control. Even if it means killing you.>

<Well . . .> Why was I making excuses for her? Why? I couldn't make any more. She wasn't my friend. She wasn't my kind.

We'd made a deal with the devil and the devil had just shown herself for what she was.

<She's gonna get us Visser Three,> I said. <Remember? That's what this is about.>

CHAPTER 17

<Careful, Ax,> I reminded him. <It's . . . well, it's worse than you said. Let the Taxxon smell the soil. Just let it dig and eat. Try not to think of us.>

<I will try to keep control of the morph,> said Ax. <As a young cadet, I researched the recorded successes and failures of Taxxon morphing. I once gave a presentation on physiological mechanisms for *notallssith*, the condition of being unable to control a morph.>

<Why didn't you tell us this before?!> Marco asked.

<The results of my research were not encouraging.>

<Oooookay.>

Ax began to morph at the opening to the tunnel that I had started. Taylor watched with fascination. I was just grossed out.

Andalite features melted into a blue-black pool until nothing was left but an oily slick. It was as if everything Andalite had to be forsaken before the Taxxon could be born.

But then, out of the pool, the beast took shape. Four round, red, jiggling eyes shook in the pool like tiny internal organs. The body grew larger and larger. It was like watching time-lapse photography of a fungus. First it grew out, flat along the floor, then up. It was hideous. The strong, beautiful Andalite body transformed and corrupted.

The bloated worm neared full size.

We waited anxiously, silent, ready.

Ax didn't move. The big Taxxon just stood there motionless, as if in a trance.

<Hey,> Jake snapped, <let's get moving.>

<Ax?> Rachel said, more kindly. <Everything all right?> She inched tentatively toward him, the way you'd approach a chained dog you didn't know.

<Give him a little nudge,> Marco suggested. He sauntered up beside Rachel, toward the big worm, his ape arms dangling loosely. He looked at Ax with exaggerated puzzlement, strolled the length of him, then announced, <It's a compre-

hensive system failure. Can't be fixed on-site. We'll have to haul this beauty back to the shop.>

<I am okay,> Ax protested, speaking at last. <I have been practicing control. By temporarily triggering Taxxon hibernation, I am able to resist the urge to eat you.>

<Thanks for telling me about hibernation before, Ax-man,> I grumbled.

<I did not understand it until now.>

<Good,> Jake said tersely. <Now dig.>

Before you could blink an eye, Ax shot down the tunnel.

<Okay,> Marco said. <So I was wrong.>

I held my breath, wanting to be sure he wasn't going to come racing back for a quick lunch. It was a good distance to where Ax was working, farther than you could see. But you could hear — no, you could feel — the sound of digging. A high-pitched, far-off ringing. The sound of teeth scraping dirt. Of dirt being devoured.

The sound sneaked up on you because it was so soft, barely audible. But it filled your head until all you could imagine was the Taxxon digging. And digging. Yard after stinking, slimy yard.

I shook my Andalite head, trying to break the trance. Beads of sweat flew off. I hadn't realized how hot it was below ground. Four large animals make a cavern oppressive.

"Did you like it, Andalite?" The voice came

from the far corner of the chamber where the gigantic steel gas main intersected it. Taylor leaned against the pipe. She was the only one who looked relaxed.

"Well?"

<Did I like what?> I said.

"Being a Taxxon, silly," she replied. "I bet you did. Some individuals are cut out to be lower life-forms."

<You'd know about that,> Rachel said angrily. <No living thing is lower than a Yeerk.> A low growl rumbled through her bared fangs.

"You know I'm right," Taylor said to Rachel. "You know this one is weak." She gestured at me.

<I'll show you weak!> Rachel slashed the air.

"You wouldn't dare. Hurt me and there's no explosion. You won't let this opportunity pass. You won't let emotions get in the way. You Andalite bandits — you're too much like us."

Rachel growled and snapped her jaws, but backed away. Taylor's words hung in my mind. This was a Yeerk plan. Every deadly detail was Yeerk. Mass destruction. No provisions to protect the innocent. That was to be expected, I guess. But we'd jumped on board.

<Is she right?> I said privately to Rachel.

<Are you crazy? The way you live, the things you do? I don't know anyone stronger. You're not weak.>

<No, not that. I mean about us being like her. Opportunists of the worse kind.>

Rachel let out a small roar. She rolled her huge head from side to side. <I'm sick and tired of this are-we-doing-the-right-thing, self-doubt crap!> she announced in thought-speak that everyone but Taylor could hear. <The Yeerks are killing people. They're destroying Earth. Hello! What's gotten into you guys? If someone starts shooting up your town and you shoot back in self-defense, do you ask if it's justified?>

Marco was uncharacteristically silent.

Jake paced back and forth, a big cat in a small, confining cage. I moved nearer to Rachel, brushing Jake in the process. He let out a repressed snarl.

<Watch it!>

<What's wrong with everybody?> Rachel asked me. <Everyone's falling apart.>

<It could be her,> I said, looking at Taylor with both stalk eyes, keeping my main eyes on Rachel. <She has a way of setting the mood. Or maybe,> I said, <maybe we're in too deep and we know it.>

<Don't talk like that. After tonight, it's going to be different. We'll fry the Yeerk pool. The balance will tip. We'll drive them out.> She was getting excited again, the way she does when she talks about the fight. But she sounded a little des-

97

perate, too. Like she needed to convince me. And herself.

<Then what?> I said.

<We could be together.> She paused. <All of us, I mean. Do normal stuff.>

<Yeah,> I said. <Rachel, do we know how many Yeerks there really are? On the Andalite home world? Invading other species? What if it's never over? Sure, maybe we pull this off today. But it doesn't change our numbers. There are still only six of us. One, two, three, four . . .>

<Stop it!> she yelled suddenly. <Tobias, I can't get the image out of my head. The way it will play out tonight. A Yeerk pool full of hosts. Humans and Hork-Bajir. They smell natural gas. They feel it pouring in. They look around, up, confused, puzzled. They start to worry. Panic. The smell gets so strong they can't breathe and they know . . . they know natural gas can blow . . . they run . . . too late. Suddenly . . . Ka-boom! A scorching, burning fireball destroys everything it touches. They're vaporized . . . Cassie was right . . .>

<They're Yeerks,> I said.

<They're humans, too.>

I thought of all the stories Ax had told us of entire planets enslaved. Of how what couldn't be enslaved was killed. Of great and peaceful societies destroyed by Yeerks.

A Yeerk was in the corner, not twenty feet away. A creature capable of the greatest evil, cowardly hiding inside a human so that no one would see the threat. How many were there now? Thousands? Fewer? More? Every day there were more human slaves. It was my first thought in the morning and my last thought before I slept.

They'd killed Elfangor, my father. The father I never knew.

The day would come when there would be no one left. An entire planet erased. I couldn't let that happen.

<They're Yeerks,> I repeated. <That's all.>

CHAPTER 18

Rachel rose on hind legs and cautiously lifted the sewer cap just enough to peer out. Standing erect, she was taller than the ceiling. She pushed the cap aside. Jake followed her out with a lightning leap. Marco brought up the rear.

Their time in morph was almost up. They needed to demorph and remorph, and Rachel needed to do a quick check-in at home. I'd been in morph about an hour and a half. Ax's turn at digging was almost up.

They put the cap partially back and disappeared. It was just Taylor and me underground.

"Your friends have left you," she observed. "What if they don't come back?"

This was part of Taylor's fun. To play with my

head. I didn't answer. I wouldn't let her affect me. When she walked slowly up to me, I didn't move. When she reached out with her real hand and touched the fur just above my shoulders, I didn't breathe.

"A handsome species," she complimented, sounding not like a teenage girl, but like a sly, sophisticated Yeerk. "You deserve more than your tradition allows."

I backed away.

"Your friends don't understand how powerful we Yeerks are," she continued. "But I know that you do. We will have no place for your friends in our new society, but you . . . every comfort you wish would be yours. We could rule together. Join us."

I jerked away, shocked that I'd let her go on so long. She laughed. A long and confident laugh.

<I thought you were moving toward democracy,> I said quietly.

"Of course we are. Of course we are. But think . . . democracies need leaders, and laws to protect the citizens. Someone has to make the laws . . ."

<It will never be me.>

"You deserve more," she persisted, then grinned, turned, and walked away. It was an odd thing to say. I felt like a doomed mouse, poked and prodded by a clawed cat. I couldn't respond. I could only look away.

A crescent of light illuminated the chamber. I heard yelping and looked up to see two wolves pawing and pushing at the heavy iron cap. They slid it open and leaped down, landing very hard.

<We wanted to be smaller,> Marco explained privately. <But we have to keep Taxxon-Ax in line, and Yeerk-girl intimidated.>

Jake paced back and forth before the tunnel opening. The new morph allowed him eight paces before he had to turn around. Better than the five in tiger. He was silent for a minute, then, looking at the watch I wore, <Guys, uh, we've got a problem. Ax was due back by now. I've been calling him, but he doesn't answer. Did you change plans, Tobias?>

<No.> I raised an arm to silence everyone. We listened. Marco pressed an ear to the side of the tunnel. I could just make out a very faint grating sound, much fainter than before. Maybe it was Andalite hearing. Or maybe Ax was . . .

<He's still going at it,> Marco announced. <The boy's gonna dig to China.>

I took a few steps into the tunnel. <Ax, can you hear me? You have to stop. You'll die of exhaustion.> There was no reply, thought-speak or otherwise. <He must be fixated. We have to stop him.>

<Just what do you have in mind?> Marco asked.

102

I looked at Taylor. She sat with her back against the wall and glanced from me to Jake to Marco with casual suspicion. I looked hesitantly at the opening of the tunnel. It wasn't really large enough for our power morphs.

<I have an idea,> I said. I took off the watch, checked the glow-in-the-dark numbers. Put it around Jake's right front leg. <Cover me.> I trotted several feet into the tunnel. When I saw, through swiveled stalk eyes, that Jake and Marco had planted themselves in front of the entrance and masked me from Taylor's view, I demorphed. Then I began to morph again.

Feathers turned to thin skin that stretched tight as an umbrella over wing bones. Blindness banished all trace of light. It had been dark already, but now there was a vision void. A nothingness that made my heart pound.

Then, a new sense. A kind of hearing. The sharpest hearing you've ever known. I couldn't make out everything, but the higher sounds were crystal clear.

Then suddenly, it was more than mere hearing. I could tell exactly where all sounds came from. They formed a picture of my surroundings. So much like sight. So different, too.

I was echolocating. I was a bat.

<Jake, Marco, follow me,> I called. I flapped my thin wings far faster than a hawk ever does

and flew easily along the tunnel. The sonic chirps I emitted told me exactly where the sides were. The bat felt at home.

<Ax?>

No answer. I flew a long way, maybe a quarter mile, until I came to something strange. The tunnel became something else, something expanded. A hollowed-out space. A large cavern-room. Like maybe Ax had gone nuts and circled up and down ten or twelve times.

I could hear Ax now. Closer. The high-pitched screeching of Taxxon teeth on dirt and small rocks was almost deafening to bat senses. Extra-loud echolocation was necessary to see over the noise. The tunnel continued on the far side of the chamber. I flapped my wings and flew in.

<Ax, is that you?> My chirps weren't returning. They were being absorbed. By something soft, something . . .

WHAP!

I flew into Ax's backside and slapped to the tunnel floor.

<Ax, stop!> I focused all my energy on that thought-speak command, trying to penetrate his trance. It worked. He stopped digging.

<Cannot go on,> he groaned faintly.

<Darn straight. You've got minutes left in morph, Ax-man. Let's clear out.>

<Too weak. Can . . . not . . . can . . . not move.>

The tunnel had narrowed to barely bigger than the circumference of the Taxxon. Usually a Taxxon's vigor made its tunnel at least large enough for it to comfortably wiggle out.

<Tobias, what's going on?> Jake, sounding understandably edgy. <We can't see anything.>

<Follow the tunnel,> I said shortly. <Ax is stuck. An overeating stupor. He's dying here with, like, seven minutes left in morph. You have to pull him out.>

<You want us to march straight toward a Taxxon? Whose side are you on?>

<He's too weak to turn around or hurt you.>

<I better get overtime for this,> Marco said. <Serious overtime.>

Marco and Jake crawled through the pitch-black until they bumped into Ax.

<Oh, man!> Marco gasped. <Wolf sense of smell is way too good.> The stench was over-whelming.

They bit into the soft baggy flesh and pulled.

"Skreeeee!" Ax cried involuntarily.

<Hurry,> I said to Jake. <There's no time!>

The hulking worm began to move. Marco strained and fought. Jake snarled and pulled. Inch by inch they dragged Ax out. By the watch

105

around Jake's leg, it took a full five minutes to reach the carved out, earthen cavern.

Less than two minutes to go.

<I think he's unconscious,> Jake said.

<His skin has no bulge. It's like he's deflating.>

<Demorph,> I urged. <Please, Ax, demorph!>

No answer.

<Ax, now!> Jake ordered.

<We were too late,> Marco said flatly. <He's going to die.>

CHAPTER 19

<Ax!> I cried. Panic gripped my tiny bat heart. <Ax! Ax! Ax!>

<Yes, Tobias. It is me.> I caught the echo of something larger and more reflective than a Taxxon. A form that was changing. Becoming taller than a wolf . . . four legs . . . two arms . . .

We collapsed in the darkness, exhausted and terrified, thankful to be together.

I demorphed and prepared to dig again as a Taxxon. But then . . .

"Hey, what's going on?"

A faint light, way down the tunnel. It was coming nearer, bobbing as it came.

Jake and Marco saw the light, too. We watched as it increased in size and brightness until at last

Taylor emerged into the earth-cavern. Rachel was in grizzly morph right behind her, her body wedged tight in the tunnel.

Taylor crawled on hands and knees in the Taxxon goo. There was no question the Yeerk was in full control. It was the kind of thing Taylor-the-girl would never do. Her hair was a mess, plastered to her face by Taxxon slime. One hand gripped an electric fluorescent lantern.

"What happened here?" Taylor demanded, looking at the cavern. When my eyes adjusted, I saw what a strange place the cavern was. It wasn't square or round or ovoid. Nothing normal. It was an undulating, chaotic intersection of many different, smaller tunnels.

<I lost control of the morph,> Ax answered honestly. <I do not remember everything. I know that I became confused. I dug and ate in circles for many minutes before regaining focus.>

<He ate himself to exhaustion,> Jake added, more for Rachel than for Taylor. <We had to drag him out.>

<I do not remember,> Ax confessed.

"Andalite incompetent," Taylor raged suddenly.

<Watch yourself, Yeerk,> Rachel roared back.

<It's okay, Ax-man,> Jake said privately. <You dug about ten times farther than we expected. Tobias, take it easy this time. And, uh, don't morph or demorph near us, okay?>

108

I didn't need to be reminded. Jake didn't want me eating them. He also didn't want Taylor seeing me morph straight from hawk to Taxxon.

I hopped to the opening of the tunnel Ax had dug and flapped a little to get out of sight. My wings scraped the tunnel sides and I crash-landed about fifty feet in.

<I'm going Taxxon,> I warned.

I was better prepared this time. I was ready when the instincts reared up and told me to follow the smell of my friends.

I turned my ravenous, empty belly to the tunnel instead. I rushed forward to the place where Ax had stopped. Fierce hunger propelled me into the soil wall.

I was more aware this time. I felt what was going on around me. What was going on inside the Taxxon mind. It wasn't simple hunger. It wasn't pure rage.

No. What drove the Taxxon to eat and dig was more complicated. It was something I understood. A sort of insecurity or fear.

Yes, a fear . . . grossly exaggerated . . . beyond anything humans experience . . . a desperate fear of not having enough . . . a terror of starvation . . . a horror that your essential needs will go unfulfilled . . . a horror demented and contorted by the Taxxon mind until it became a sick, murderous evil.

I wouldn't have understood, or even noticed, if I hadn't been hawk for so long. I've experienced just enough of that feeling to recognize it.

A whole species of terrified overeaters. It made me almost sorry for them.

Almost.

I dug and thought of Taylor. The Yeerk and the girl. What they'd let themselves become . . .

Was anyone all evil? That couldn't be possible. I've heard that even Hitler was good to his dogs.

Taylor had been too insecure to face her peers without her beauty. She'd done what she had to do to make the fear go away.

Evil, even the worst evil, has banal origins every human can understand.

Weakness. Fear. Insecurity.

I understood Taylor. I understood the Taxxon.

The realization frightened me as nothing ever has.

Suddenly, the Taxxon's pace began to slow. I was getting tired, if you can call it that. A digging Taxxon doesn't get tired the way people do. It doesn't notice it's tired. It doesn't decide to slow. It just fades away, like a drained battery.

I'd lost track of time. Must have been digging for over an hour. I pressed on. Eating. Expelling. The dirt tasted good. It wasn't flesh, but it wasn't bad.

Soon there were more and more rocks in the dirt. Small at first, then larger. Bigger than even a Taxxon could swallow. I pushed the rocks aside and continued until I hit a smooth, continuous surface. Probably the remnants of an old building foundation.

I tried to go around. It curved up and up, like the crest of a dome.

Then it hit me. I'd reached it. I'd found the Yeerk pool.

I continued along the surface until it became almost flat and I found what I thought was the top. Taylor said we would strike fairly high. I never guessed we would strike at the center.

There were no cracks or openings anywhere. It was completely continuous. How could I break through?

The Taxxon knew what to do.

I opened my Taxxon mouth wide. Full capacity. I swiveled my teeth so they scraped the concrete like a drill. A hundred teeth screeched across the stone. Friction made my mouth hot. Caustic Taxxon spit burned and dissolved the rock.

I gnawed deep into the shell of the dome, a hole four or more feet across and almost as deep. My body felt heavy and ill. And at last I saw a flicker of red light.

CHAPTER 20

A thousand horrors. A crazy, mixed-up hell right here on Earth. A melting pot of enslaved, alien races. A sea of two kinds of motion: the slow, deliberate movements of bodies who aren't free, and the wild, desperate spasms of doomed, caged prisoners.

From my vantage point, the pool itself churned directly below. Hard to say how far down. Not more than a hundred feet. Then there was the infestation pier, built out above the slugs. Human after human cursed or spit or wailed before the Hork-Bajir forced their head under to accept a Yeerk master.

The cages that ringed the pool seemed to

have multiplied since I'd seen them last. It was like a bizarre sort of amphitheater. The spectators were the people from town. Some of them I knew. Like Ms. Powell, my old math teacher, and Brent Starr, the anchor from the news.

Others were strangers to me. Mothers and fathers. Young kids. Bus drivers. Lawyers. Artists. Government employees. Everyone, from every walk of life. All screaming. Burning out their vocal cords. Tears pouring from eyes. Veins bulging from foreheads. Sweat coursing from brows.

They wanted to be free! They wanted nothing more than to be free.

Then I realized that a great number of the caged prisoners weren't crying out. They watched the proceedings with distaste, but they didn't rage with anger. They stood immobile and calm. I'd seen voluntary hosts before. Voluntary hosts enjoyed the show. These weren't voluntary.

Who were they? What had happened to these hosts? It was like they'd passed a point beyond the point of caring. Like they were zombies or something. But that was impossible. Everyone fights for freedom to the bitter end. Everyone has to!

These hosts had an air about them. They stared off into the vast space with a look of . . . pride? Conviction? They looked almost as if they had purpose.

Maybe they were Yeerks from the peace faction? So many of them here? Now? Oh, man, not now . . .

"Beautiful, isn't it?" whispered a female voice inches from my head. I jerked against the tunnel wall.

It was Taylor. Taylor!

How did she crawl down the tunnel alone? How did she get away from the others?

Who cared?

Every inch of me wanted to bite her head off. She was a fleshy meal ready-made. Plus, she was the scum of the universe. Would it be so bad to get rid of her?

I opened my mouth, moved in for the attack . . .

And was suddenly paralyzed. I couldn't move my mouthparts or upper body. How stupid was I? She'd zapped me.

"Don't be dumb," she said. "Get control of your morph."

Ax had said something about a hibernation state. I searched the Taxxon consciousness for a clue. I found it suddenly in a mental vision, an image of bodies mounded into an endless mountain. The picture relaxed me. I could feast forever. I didn't have to find food, I had enough right there.

I was in control enough to speak.

114

<How did you get here? The others would never let you walk away from them.>

"You don't think they trust me? I'm hurt. Really."

<What did you do to them?>

"You know me, Andalite. I wouldn't hurt a fly. I temporarily incapacitated them, yes. I needed to talk to you."

<We're in,> I said. I began now to broadcast my thought-speak, hoping the others would hear me, wherever they were.

"I can see that," she mocked. "But I don't care right now. I want to talk to you." I stayed quiet. I felt sick. It wasn't the Taxxon's problem. It was mine. Taylor had me cornered.

"Relax," she continued. "You're shaking like one of Visser Three's personal guards. It's just me. Remember me?"

<What do you want?> I asked.

"Look down there," she said, glancing at the Yeerk pool. "We are so organized. We run with the precision of a Swiss watch. We are invincible. When I take command, we will reach new heights."

<What are you talking about? Take command? You mean, when you introduce democracy.>

"Yes, of course that's what I mean," she said, the corners of her mouth turning upward with a shocking lack of subtlety. "I want you to join me. I think you know how smart I am. I think you

115

know my will to succeed. I want you to cofound the new Yeerk society."

Suddenly, Taylor's words seemed distant. Because I saw the hidden spot, down by the Yeerk pool. I saw the place where I had perched as the seconds counted down. The seconds before I became a *nothlit.*

"What do you get as an underling with Andalite bandits?" she went on, her voice seductive. "You are obviously not a leader. You are not even second-in-command. You are a nobody."

I flashed back to that night at the Yeerk pool. Remembered how carefully I had weighed my options. Since then I'd been telling myself there was no choice. That if I'd demorphed, the visser would have been on me in a flash. He would have known that we were human. He would have found my friends.

But there is always a choice. In any and every situation. It's usually the choice between bad and worse. But it's still a choice.

"Come on," she said again. "Be my host. Offer me your body and you can have anything you want."

Choice. Traitor or . . .

<Can I have freedom?> I asked.

"It is a kind of freedom," she answered.

<Can I be happy?> I asked.

"It is a kind of happiness," she replied.

I looked back at the rock face, my *nothlit* birthplace. I'd made a decision. Had I made a bad decision? I didn't know. And suddenly, I realized that I would never know. I know that I stuck with my choice. And that I had followed it through to the very end.

I looked at Taylor. For the first time, her physical beauty was difficult to see. Her hair and face were covered in dirt. Her expression was the twisted, power-hungry look of a dictator. The only thing that could have made her beautiful now was her inside. And there certainly wasn't anything beautiful there.

<I'm stronger than that,> I said slowly. <You're only out for power and control. That's it. And when you get it — *if* you get it — you'll only want more. I think that power as your only goal is pointless.>

"You don't really believe that," she mocked.

<Don't I?> I said. <If I didn't, why would I find you so gross? How would I see that you're weak? All you're about is envy and power.>

She looked at me, then at the pool, then back down the tunnel. "And it will be my pleasure," she rasped, "to prove you right."

CHAPTER 21

She jabbed her synthetic fist in my still-paralyzed throat and left me gagging. Then she turned away from the view of the Yeerk pool and shot off down the tunnel as fast as human legs would carry her.

<Where are you going?> I choked out. Her lantern disappeared from view.

"You'll know soon enough, Andalite!" she cried.

I shed all thoughts of hibernation and summoned the hunger that had been sitting on the edge of my consciousness.

I focused on the image of the girl and my legs began to scratch and scrape against the rocky tunnel walls. I squished my body into an impossible U-shape. I needed to turn around. Sure, I

118

could run just as fast backward. But I wanted my mouth, my weapon, to be ready.

I called again. <Stop!>

No answer.

I powered my legs like there was a raw T-bone six inches from my face. With the speed of a greyhound and the mass of a tree trunk, I skittered into blackness, after my prey.

My throat and neck were still numb. My tongue dangled from my mouth like a three-foot leash.

<Hey!> I called to the others. <Taylor's coming back through. Stop her!>

My needle-legs continued to scrape through the dirt, like the gallop of a hundred tiny horses.

<We can't move!> Jake yelled to me. <How long does this stuff last?>

<Not long. Try. Try!>

<Here she comes,> Rachel yelled. <Here she comes!>

<Get her!>

<We can't!>

Whoooomp!

My body burst from the tunnel like a cork from a bottle. I was in the cavern Ax had carved out. I slowed just enough to catch sight of the others. An Andalite, two wolves, and a bear, sprawled on the floor like they were taking a nap.

<Go!> Rachel cried.

I crossed the cavern and dove into the tunnel's first half. I knew I was close. I could smell her shampoo.

I was close. Her footfalls thumped the tunnel floor. Faint lantern light filled the darkness. Then more.

<Stop!> I cried.

"Never!" she screamed.

I saw Taylor's form, and then I saw beyond her. The sewer chamber was just yards ahead. Her lantern reflected off the pipeline's polished steel.

I suddenly knew what she meant to do.

<No!> I lunged. Missed. I lunged again. Full feeling returned to my mouth.

"Arghhh!" she cried. I clamped down on her heel. Not hard enough to sever her foot, but hard enough for her to feel that I was in control. Shark teeth? Bear fangs? Neither comes close to inflicting the kind of agony a Taxxon inflicts.

"Worm! Slime! Get off me!" With her real arm, she punched my face. Only a distraction. Out of the corner of one eye I saw a flash — her fake arm, her fake fingers.

I released her foot, and twisted the upper third of my body so that it slapped her artificial arm. Paralyzing particulates shot from her fingers. But not at me. They were wasted, flung at the far wall.

"Scum!" She was free and running for the pipeline. I revved my feet and shot forward.

"Stop right there!" she cried. "Come an inch closer and I'll blow a hole through this steel."

I froze.

<You said that once the tunnel was dug, we'd have twenty minutes to get away.>

"You believed me?"

<I did and I do,> I lied. <You can't blow a hole in that pipe because you know. You know that if we die in this explosion, you die, too.>

Her lips twisted into the now-familiar fiendish smile. Pure Yeerk and proud of it. "Wrong, Andalite. You forget that I am not bound to this body. I am the Yeerk inside. And a skull entirely replaced, bone by bone, by heat-proof, blast-proof polymer protects me. This body will burn, but I will survive."

I heard movement behind me. I glanced back. It was Rachel in the lead, followed by the others. Dragging their still partially paralyzed bodies out of the tunnel and into the sewer chamber.

<Get her!> Rachel cried. <Tobias, get her!>

Taylor's smile broadened. She turned toward the pipeline. She extended her artificial arm.

<No!> Rachel yelled.

Taylor blew a hole clean through the metal. And in an instant, reality changed.

121

Fwooooosh!

A pressure wave of natural gas shot from the pipe. It ripped across the chamber and sent us tumbling through the air. Taylor. Me. The others.

Tumbling . . .

Straight for the tunnel!

<Ahhhh!>

Taylor blew right past me, propelled by the gas, a swirl of blond hair and pink flesh.

And she was laughing.

CHAPTER 22

FweeeeWOOOOOOOOOSH!

The force of a fire hose. A hurricane.

<Ahhhhhh!>

We were shoved down the tunnel at breakneck speed. We slapped the sides. Slipped on slime. Gasped for air.

We were absolutely powerless!

Dirt scratched my tender eyes, blinded me.

Bammm!

I slammed the dirt wall. It knocked the wind out of me so I couldn't breathe, couldn't think.

<I cannot . . . stop!> Ax exclaimed.

<Grab onto each other,> Jake yelled. <Bite into each other. Anything!>

<No air!> Rachel gasped.

123

The tunnel was narrowing. The Yeerk pool was near. I was farthest down the tunnel, out in front. We were going to fly from a hole in the dome with me in the lead. We were going to burst from the opening. BASE jumpers with no chutes.

We were going to die.

It would end for me where it had all begun. That cavernous hell. In seconds, we'd be five blobs on the pavement, gobbled up by Taxxon guards.

Ba-BAMMM!

Marco slammed into my rump.

<Ugh!>

Jake plowed into Marco. Rachel plowed into Jake.

KA-bam!

Ax careened into Jake's rib cage, crushing him. Crushing us all.

My legs, dozens of sharp sticks, scraped the tunnel sides. I stretched them out as far as they would open. Strained to make them catch hold.

<Can't breathe!> Marco gasped.

Acute pain shot to my core. Momentum snapped off my legs. I was insane to think I could stop us! It was like trying to stop a car traveling seventy by opening the door and dragging your foot on the pavement. Not happening.

But I had a hundred legs. And the tunnel was narrowing.

<I see light!> I yelled. There it was. The red

circle that glowed like a harvest moon. Coming nearer and nearer. It was now. Or it was never.

<Ahhhhh!> I cried, and dug in what legs I had left. They punctured the dirt, scraped the stone, snapped like twigs.

"Skreeeeeeyaaaaaa!" A shrill scream from the Taxxon. A primal yelp of despair.

But the legs were slowing me. They were slowing us!

Still, the force of the gas, of the others pressing against me — I'd explode! I was a balloon about to pop. My thin skin was being pushed to the limit . . .

But the pressure of the wall was slowing us down.

I felt blood vessels fail, blood course into my eyes. My head was even with the Yeerk pool hole. It was all a blur. We inched forward, against our will. Sheer agony. The march toward death.

<Can . . . not . . . breathe,> Ax whispered.

Six inches, five inches, four inches . . .

Four inches and holding.

The pressure didn't push us any farther. It eased. And then it disappeared.

No one said anything. I called to them. Their one-word answers came in gasps. We all needed air.

<Move, guys. Move!> I said. <We have to get back.> I twisted my massive body up and around

and only then did I realize that the Taxxon was less affected by the gas. My alien physiology let me breathe in the noxious environment.

<Lungs . . . burning!> Jake sighed.

Their bodies, dark forms in the dim, distant light from the Yeerk pool, straggled lethargically along the tunnel.

<I can't,> Rachel said slowly.

<You have to!> I said. Marco dropped to the floor. The others stumbled like drunks. They weren't going to make it.

The tunnel was slick with Taxxon slime. I decided to use it for the one thing it was good for.

<C'mon!> I roared, then I charged. I plowed into them and pushed them along. Slowly at first, then faster and faster.

My hunger reemerged.

There they were. Four weak, dying animals. Mine for the feasting. Their smells. Their warmth.

It was the hardest thing I've ever done.

<They're not food,> I chanted. <They're not food.>

The legs I had left were on fire. My hunger was alive. I slid my friends along the tunnel with my big Taxxon head.

<They're not food!> I screamed.

After far too long, the dirt gave way to concrete. It was the sewer chamber.

We'd made it.

CHAPTER 23

We were conscious. We were breathing. We were alive.

Barely.

No one needed to say, <Demorph.> No thought had ever been stronger in my mind.

"The gas is off." Those were the first words out of Jake's mouth when he'd finished demorphing, the only words anyone managed to form. "How?" he whispered. He stood for a minute, numb and dazed. Incredulous. "How?"

Silently, we followed Jake up and out of the sewer chamber. He began to remorph to peregrine falcon. Marco, Rachel, and Ax followed his lead, went raptor.

<Let's go,> Jake commanded.

127

There was only one place the gas could have been turned off.

The pumping station.

I got a funny feeling as we got closer to it. Flashing lights by the doors and on the roof doused the surrounding trees in red. I knew something was up, the way you do when a police car rockets past you on the street, no sirens, but lights flashing. There was definitely trouble.

The others landed behind the bushes where Ax and I had morphed earlier. They demorphed, crouching low as their bodies rose from the earth. And even though I knew they were all exhausted, they slowly morphed again. Battle morphs. We weren't taking any chances.

The plate glass door was shattered. A thousand shards sparkled on the sidewalk.

<Somebody charged this place,> I said. <Somebody wild.>

<Come on. Who'd break into a pumping station? No cash. No goods,> Marco said.

<Maybe their gas bill was too much to take,> Rachel answered.

The others stole along the perimeter single file, an absurd and unlikely circus troupe. I circled above. No one hiding in the bushes. No snipers posted on the roof.

<Weird,> I said. <I don't see anyone.> I

landed on the pavement, morphed Andalite, and joined the others. We crunched over glass and stepped through what was left of the door frame. Moved into the building.

<Oh, man,> I heard Rachel say. <Oh, man!>

I stepped around her. My rear legs weakened.

Then I saw the bodies. Human bodies. Maybe half a dozen. Male and female. Suited to look like gas company workers.

Sprawled now every which way. They were alive — barely. They'd obviously been on the losing end of one very fierce battle. None seemed conscious.

Yeerk slugs wriggled and writhed helplessly on the floor.

<Who could have done this?> Jake gasped.

<I think *why* is the better question,> Marco added.

<Taylor,> Rachel said, her voice grim. <But no, that's impossible. 'Cause she was with us. This was her plan and she needed these people. Visser Three?>

I moved forward, stepping carefully over the bodies with my four legs. I heard a police siren wail in the distance and I knew. I knew they were coming here. Maybe real cops. Maybe Controller-cops. It didn't matter. No time either way. We had to get out.

129

But I kept going. I kept going because before the siren wailed, I'd heard a noise. A sound of life farther on in the building.

<Tobias, we've gotta get out of here. We're not going to figure this out,> Rachel said. <At least not now.>

I didn't turn back. I moved into the guts of the building, where compressors and pumps that once hummed smoothly sat silent and immobile.

I followed the sound. There was a door to what looked like a little office. I peered in.

And then I saw her, sitting with her elbows on a table, her head in her hands.

Cassie. Crying.

She had turned off the gas and saved our lives. She had done this.

<Cassie, it's me.> She didn't look up. She didn't move. <Cassie.>

With delicate Andalite arms, I tried to lift her from the chair. She stood but was limp in my arms.

<C'mon, Cassie. We have to get out of here. It's okay. Everything's okay.>

Her sobs stopped. Halting half-gasps took their place. She turned in my arms, turned so that she stood and faced me. Her eyes, red and wet, stared up at mine. Salt streaks dried on her face.

"No," she said. "It will never be okay."

CHAPTER 24

It was the next day. The sun beat down. And produced columns of rising hot air. I must have gone twelve minutes without flapping a wing. Rachel, too. Nature was giving us a free ride.

We were way up. So high. You can't even see prey from that height. But what's cool is that we weren't the only birds up there. I guess true hawks need to get away, too, sometimes.

Why? I don't know. Maybe they need the perspective. Maybe they need to feel that they're not tied to the world of their meadow. Maybe they're pushing the boundaries, seeing how high they can sail before the air gets too thin.

Or maybe they don't know why they do anything.

<The beach?> Rachel called.

<Yeah. How about the cove?> We turned like fighter planes and pulled out of our ascent. The trees and hills raced toward us, the ocean frothed not far beyond.

I thought of the sinkhole where Bobby nearly drowned. The dirt flat where his father gripped him lovingly.

I spotted the pumping station as we descended. It was roped off by caution tape. Still buzzing with cops and investigators.

I thought of the last second in which I'd seen Taylor, blown through the tunnel, Barbie doll hair streaming. Her image remained but her voice was gone. Maybe just for now, maybe forever. Too soon to tell.

The cove is the closest thing to a secret beach that we know about. It's all jutting rocks and twenty-foot drops to the sea, so it's not too popular with the regular beach crowd. You practically have to be a bird to get to it.

Rachel demorphed and I morphed to my human self. The sun was warm. The air was salty. We were together.

"There was no way we could have known," she said, sensing my mood, knowing where my mind was. "We were acting on the best information we had."

"I'm not sure," I said. "Did you talk to Cassie? Did she tell you what happened?"

"Yeah. Jake took her home last night, but I stopped by this morning."

"Well?"

"She contacted Tidwell because Jake said she could warn him. While we were digging the tunnel, Cassie talked to the Yeerk peace faction. Guess what Tidwell told her?"

I raised my eyebrows.

"Tidwell and all the peacenik Yeerks try to feed at the same time. They try to show up at the Yeerk pool together so they can exchange information and make plans."

"We know that," I interrupted.

"Right. But we didn't know that they'd reorganized their feeding schedule. We didn't know that they'd rescheduled so they'd predominate on Saturday afternoons."

There was a long pause as I calculated just what that meant.

"Somehow Visser Three got the news? He was going to kill off all his opposition in one day! The Andalite bandits. The Yeerk peace faction. Two groups, one plan."

"Yeah. And Cassie thinks he wanted more than our lives," she said. "She thinks Visser Three planned to pin the atrocity on the peace

133

faction. That he was going to weaken them by frying all their hosts, then discredit them by making it look like they were responsible for arranging the gas explosion and for engineering massive loss of Yeerk life."

"That sounds like the visser we know and love."

"And if he sacrificed some innocent Yeerks along the way," Rachel continued, "it would be a small price for a plan that would also, thanks to Taylor, annihilate us."

"So Taylor was working with Visser Three all along. She pretended to be against him to get us to cooperate." I took a deep breath over the pain in my chest. "After all the clues! All the gut feelings! I don't believe I didn't see more clearly. I should have looked at the bigger picture . . ."

"Hey. No matter what you think, Tobias, Taylor's not your responsibility. Besides, how often is it possible to see the big picture, really?" Rachel said. "Things happen fast. You just have to make the best decision you can and then go for it. You know what? I'd do the same thing again, if I had to."

"How can you say that?"

"With me, it's about instinct. I knew we had to dig that tunnel. Turns out I was right, but for the wrong reasons. If we hadn't gotten involved with Taylor, Cassie wouldn't have known about the plan, wouldn't have talked to Tidwell, wouldn't have worried about us. But she did. And it opened up a course of events that couldn't have occurred otherwise. It ended up saving the Yeerk peace faction. It was a good investment."

"Cassie battled a bunch of humans. Alone. You're saying that's a good thing?"

"Of course not," Rachel said emphatically. "But it was the lesser of two evils."

I sat down on a rock slab. The waves crashed. The wind whipped. Rachel sat down next to me.

Maybe I was weak, but at least I was free. My choices were my own. No matter what.

Was it over for Taylor? Did she blow through the hole in the Yeerk pool dome? Lodge in a crevice of the tunnel till the gas pressure died? Catch a crag of rock and hang on? Did she live? Would Taylor-the-girl ever live again?

Would I ever stop caring?

"You never really know how some things will turn out," I said. A twig blew across the surface of a rock, swept along by the wind. I reached out to catch it. Rachel moved to stop it, too. Our hands collided gently. I took her hand. The twig blew past us, and fell into a crack.

"Yeah," she answered, smiling. "There's no real point in worrying about what you might have done. The past is the past, Tobias. Let it go."

#44 The Unexpected

I screamed.

He screamed.

His dog flattened himself against the ground in front of his master and let out a low growl.

I crept backward in the dirt.

"It's okay, Tjala." The kid reached out to scratch the dog's neck. He glanced up at me, then lowered his eyes. "He won't bite you," he said.

The kid was about my age, maybe older. It was hard to tell in the moonlight. He'd been sitting between a big rock and a clump of bushes, and I'd practically landed in his lap when I'd climbed out of the ravine. His skin was dark, darker than mine. He dissolved into the night shadows.

I glanced around. What else was lurking in the dark?

"No worries," he said. "We are alone."

I glanced around again, not sure whether or not to believe him. "Man," I said. "You scared me."

"I scared *you*?" He laughed. His dark curls bobbed. The dog's ears twitched. "That's funny."

"Yeah. Hysterical." I pulled myself out of the dirt and started to brush off my clothes. I peeked up at the kid and caught him staring at my leotard.

He looked quickly away.

I glanced down. Okay, so the thing was in shreds. Rachel would be thrilled. She'd get to take me shopping for a new one when I got home.

If I got home. I looked up. "Um —"

The kid smiled. "You'll be needing some help."

"Uh. yeah."

What was it with him? It was like he was reading my mind. His voice was soft, and a little shy, but also confident. Like he knew what needed to be done and was willing to do it. Kind of like . . . Jake.

I shook my head. No, nothing like Jake.

"Yeah, I could use some help. I'm sort of —" Gee, how was I going to explain suddenly appearing out of nowhere? "Lost."

"Lost." He laughed again. "The bird-girl who can change into a bug is lost. No worries. Now you're found. . . ."

A Fight Down Under

ANIMORPHS®

K. A. Applegate

After a mission backfires, Cassie ends up stranded in the Australian Outback. She's in the middle of nowhere, but she's not alone. She's got Visser Three for company.

ANIMORPHS #44: THE UNEXPECTED

Coming This July Wherever Books Are Sold

Visit the Web site at: www.scholastic.com/animorphs

ANIT700

AПIMORPHƧ

K. A. Applegate